DAVE HANNIGAN is an award-winning journalist, author and retired corner-forward. Born and reared in Cork, he now lives in Rocky Point, New York with his wife Cathy and sons Abe and Charlie. He often wishes he could still play Gaelic football the way he did when he was ten. Dave has written four books for adults; *Kicking On* is his first book for children.

DAVE HANNIGAN

THE O'BRIEN PRESS
DUBLIN

First published 2010 by The O'Brien Press Ltd,
12 Terenure Road East, Rathgar, Dublin 6, Ireland.
Tel: +353 1 4923333; Fax: +353 1 4922777
E-mail: books@obrien.ie
Website: www.obrien.ie

ISBN: 978-1-84717-189-4

British Library Cataloguing in Publication Data
A catalogue record for this title is available from the British Library

1 2 3 4 5 6 7 8
10 11 12 13

The O'Brien Press receives
assistance from

Layout and design: The O'Brien Press Ltd
Printed and bound in the UK by JF Print Ltd, Sparkford, Somerset.
The paper in this book is produced using pulp from managed forests.

Front cover photo © copyright Sportsfile.
Football cover images © copyright iStockphoto.

To my son, Abe

Acknowledgements

For their assistance in various ways with this book, I would like to sincerely thank my friends Gavin O'Connor and Denis Walsh, my wife Cathy Frost and my editor Helen Carr. Most of all, I want to express my gratitude to my darling boys, Abe and Charlie, one for reading and improving every chapter with his suggestions, the other for getting me up at five every morning with his smile.

PROLOGUE

... with three seconds remaining in the Super Bowl, it falls to the New York Giants' place-kicker, Shaun Reedy. He's sprinting on to the field now and all of America is watching. If he can convert this forty-two yard field goal, he will win his team the world championship. Calm as you like, he's swinging that trusty right foot back and forth as he warms up. His team is trailing by two points. He's got the chance to kick three. He looks very composed and why wouldn't he? He hasn't missed a field goal from any distance in over a year... The ball is snapped ... He's kicked it ... It has the height ... It looks good ... but no, it's gone left and wide. A matter of inches. But wide ... oh so wide ... Reedy has collapsed on the field ... Not a single team-mate has even walked to console him ... He's just lying there with his face in his hands ... wondering where it all went wrong.

CHAPTER ONE

Peter O'Connor knew every car in the village. Not only the make. He knew most of the licence plates too. The rest of the kids often wondered whether he had a notebook where he jotted all this information down. But no, it was in his head. That was his thing.

Inevitably then, he was the first one to spot the strange car pulling up outside the fence during training that Saturday morning. The rest were too obsessed with a game of backs and forwards to notice anything. Not Peter though. Just at the time he was supposed to be marking Johnny Delaney, he was walking towards the fence to get a better look.

He came back – after Johnny had been allowed to kick a nice point untouched – to break the news to the others.

'It's a stranger in a Ford Focus,' he said to no-one in particular. 'Never saw him before.

2008 D reg. Probably a rental car.'

Most of them half-turned to check out the visitor. Dinny Murphy, the long-serving manager of the Dromtarry Gaelic Football Club Under-11s, a man known to everybody in the village as Murph, just shook his head.

'Thanks for the update Peter,' he said. 'You'll make a great guard someday. Now, can you get back to corner-back and try to remember you're supposed to be marking Johnny?'

With a week to go before the first match of the season, the last thing Murph needed was any distraction like this. After four long, sometimes very long, decades training kids, he knew it only took the slightest thing to take their minds completely off the game.

'I wonder who this fella is though, and why is he watching our training?' asked Davey McCarthy. Centre-fielder. The tallest player on the team. The best player on the team. Usually the most-focused player at training too.

'He might be a tourist, just taking in the show

we put on here at training,' said Peter, loving the fact his best friend Davey had got involved in the distraction.

'My Dad says we don't get tourists here unless they're lost,' reckoned Johnny Delaney. 'I think he might be a scout from Kilturk, sent over to see if we are any good.'

'Can you ignore that car now please?' pleaded Murph.

They couldn't. Their concentration had been broken. Even Charlie Morrissey had walked out from the goal to see if he was missing anything important.

By then, Peter was offering a more detailed description of the car and trying to convince the others that the driver had just waved at him.

'Ah lads, please, can we forget about the car?' asked Murph again. He was squeezing a battered O'Neill's ball so hard between his knotted hands it looked like it might burst. 'Is it any wonder my hair is grey with this kind of carry-on?'

'But you've always been grey, Murph,' chipped in Johnny Delaney, a cheeky corner-forward with or without the ball in his hands.

'Yeah,' said Davey, 'my Dad says you were grey when you coached him and that was twenty-five years ago.'

This brought them on to one of their favourite subjects.

'How old are you anyway, Murph?' asked Peter. A question always guaranteed to get Murph annoyed and to make everybody else laugh.

'Is it true you're the oldest fella in charge of a team in Ireland?' asked Peter, loving the laughter the first question had brought.

'I'm older than God and twice as powerful,' he replied. 'Now Peter, you can lead the whole team on a lap of the field there to try and get your brains back into focus.'

Off they trotted. They hadn't gone twenty metres when the Ford Focus revved up at the far end of the fence and headed out of town and up a hill known as Baker's Lane. Peter saw this, pressed on his own brakes and brought the whole squad to a halt.

'Murph, did you see where the car went?' Peter shouted back to Murph.

'Yes I did, Peter, I also see you stopped running,' said the long-suffering manager.

'There's nothing up that hill only the old Reedy house and nobody's lived there for years.'

'Donkey's years,' said Murph who all of a sudden didn't seem as annoyed at the interruption.

'They say it's haunted you know,' said Peter.

'They do say that,' said Murph. He paused and looked off in the direction in which the car had gone. 'But that's not true. That's a load of old rubbish. Now, would you ever please get back to the running and do a lap of this field for me?'

Slowly, Peter and the rest of the players began to jog again.

CHAPTER TWO

On the way to school that Monday morning, Peter O'Connor and Davey McCarthy had just turned on to the Main Street when they saw the very same Ford Focus. It was parked outside the Spar. Too good a chance to pass up.

They just had to wait to see if the stranger would emerge.

'We're going to be late,' said Davey after they'd been standing two minutes by the crooked signpost for which Dromtarry was famous.

'No, we're not,' replied Peter. 'We've loads of time yet.'

'We still look like right fools just standing around here.'

'Sssh, here he comes.'

A man had indeed come out of the shop. A fit-looking man with a couple of bulging plastic bags in both hands. Peter grew all excited at the sight.

'He's an American, has to be,' he said.

'Why?' asked Davey.

'He's wearing a baseball cap for starters.'

'Loads of people wear baseball caps,' said Davey, growing increasingly worried that this spying episode was going to make him late for school for the first time in his life.

'Nah, that's a real one, like the one my aunt brought me back when she went shopping in New York last year,' said Peter, already moving across the street as the car pulled away. 'There's only one way to settle this one. We'll go in and ask Paudie.'

Paudie Sweeney ran the Spar, owned the garage at the top of the town, and sponsored the jerseys for the Dromtarry Under-11s. He also loved nothing more than kids coming into the shop asking him questions. The moment he saw the pair of schoolboys before him his eyes lit up.

'Well, if it isn't the men. What can I get ye, boys?'

'Eh, nothing really, Paudie, we just want to know something.' Peter was doing the talking. Davey was just standing there, looking at his watch, half-embarrassed that he'd been dragged into his friend's new obsession.

'Go on.'

'Who was that fella who was just in here?' asked Peter.

'What fella?' Paudie was making fun of them. They knew that much because he turned around as he said it, pretending to fix something on the wall behind him. Peter played along.

'You know … tall … wearing a baseball cap?

'Oh, that fella. A strange character alright.'

Paudie was adjusting his cash register now, wearing a smirk and looking over the boys' heads at the doorway.

'An American chap. Gave his name as Wayne, John Wayne. Says he's in town for a while on his way out west.'

He was sniggering as he spoke. Peter and

Davey could see that, but they couldn't figure out why. They had left the shop and were hurrying towards the school gates when Davey finally got the joke. He stopped walking and started smacking himself on the forehead.

'I know exactly who John Wayne is,' he said. 'He's an actor. He always plays cowboys in black and white films. My granddad makes me watch them on Sunday afternoons if he comes over to our house.'

'You mean that's not the fella's real name?' said Peter.

'Well, obviously, unless he's his son! That was just Paudie having a bit of fun off us.'

The school bell rang in the yard and a hundred kids suddenly began to pour from all corners towards the front doors.

'We're no nearer to solving the mystery then,' said Peter. 'We do know he's an American though and he's staying somewhere around here. Maybe he'll turn up to watch training again this Saturday.'

Peter turned to see what Davey thought of that idea but he was talking to fresh air by then. His friend was already sprinting across the now-empty tarmac towards school.

CHAPTER THREE

In the dressing-room before training, the talk was always the same. Who had been put out in the corridor for messing in school? Who got the most homework? Who had the toughest teacher? And, who, just who, was responsible for the awful smell of toe-jam that had been there since the first time any of them had walked in the door to tog off. This particular Saturday, the pong seemed milder than usual. That may have been because everybody was too excited to notice. The first match of the year was just twenty-four hours away.

After three weeks of endless games of backs and forwards, the real thing was drawing near. They could all sense it in Murph's voice when he rang around the houses earlier in the week to remind them to be on time for what he called 'the dress-rehearsal'.

Still, Charlie Morrissey was just sauntering in

the door when Peter and Davey were walking out onto the field, already togged out.

'Your pal is here,' said Charlie, gesturing over his shoulder with his gear bag.

'What pal?'

'The Yank.'

Charlie was right. There he was, baseball cap and all, standing deep in conversation with Murph by one of the goalposts.

In the five days since the incident outside Paudie Sweeney's shop, Peter hadn't even thought about the stranger. Well, apart from that time during computer lab when he asked Davey whether he should Google John Wayne just to be sure it really was an actor's name.

Now the international man of mystery was laughing and joking with Murph. They were slapping each other on the arms. Shaking their heads the way adults do when they think something is too funny. It was like they were best friends all of a sudden.

That was the last thought to go through

Peter's mind when everything went black.

Boosh!!!

He'd been so taken with the sight of the stranger that he'd wandered right into the goal-mouth. Deaf to the cries of his team-mates, he'd taken a Johnny Delaney pile-driver right to the side of the head. Then he'd crumpled in a heap.

'He's not out cold,' announced Murph who'd raced to his side. 'He's just a little groggy.'

Not too groggy. He still noticed who was standing in the crowd hovering over him as he lay on the dewy grass.

'You ... You're ... you're the Am ... American.'

Everybody laughed. Even the American.

'Yes I am,' replied the man in the baseball cap. 'Guilty as charged.'

As was the ritual, once it became apparent the injury wasn't serious, the rest of the team became more amused than concerned.

'I thought there'd be birds flying around his heads like in the cartoons,' said Davey as he watched Murph tend to his injured friend.

'The sound-effects weren't exactly WWE-standard either,' remarked Charlie Morrissey, Cork's number one wrestling fan.

'It might help if you guys moved back to give him some air,' said the American. He was standing amongst them now and they noticed a couple of things. He spoke like every television character they knew and he had the thickest legs they'd ever seen in shorts.

Maybe it was the accent. Perhaps it was the size of the legs. But they moved back quickly and gave Murph room to bring Peter back to the land of the living.

At a safe distance, of course, they began to gossip.

'He has legs like tree trunks. Did ya see them?'

'He reminds me of John Cena.'

'What about the accent? He talks like something off the television. Maybe he's from Nickelodeon?'

'Sorry guys, that's the only accent I have.'

The American was suddenly standing in amongst them now, bouncing a ball and smiling at their comments. He had the whitest teeth they'd ever seen. One more thing they'd all talk about later.

'So, you guys ready for the Balleer Bryckery boys tomorrow?' His mangled pronounciation of the name of their first opponents drew a few muffled laughs and swapped glances.

'They're called Ballybricker actually,' said Davey, his head down as he spoke.

By then, nobody was listening anyway. The American had begun rolling the ball on his pointer finger, basketball-style. Every high-speed turn mesmerised the boys more and more.

'I see you're putting on some entertainment for the troops,' said Murph, flicking the ball back into his own hands to the delight of his team.

'I am,' replied the American.

'Well, I think it's about time I introduced you.

Lads, I'd like you all to meet Shaun Reedy.'

The American made an elaborate bow in their direction at the mention of his name.

'Shaun is the son of a very old friend of mine. Shaun's father left Dromtarry for America a long time ago and he's back to stay in the town for a few weeks.'

If Peter O'Connor's eyes lit up as he downloaded all that information, they were positively bulging at what came next.

'Shaun has played a bit of sport over in New York and, if it's alright with ye boys, he's going to help me out with the team for a few weeks.'

'Is he going to be your assistant?' asked Johnny Delaney.

'Exactly,' said Murph. 'That's what he is. My assistant. And after forty-odd years, it's about time they gave me one.'

CHAPTER FOUR

By half-time in the Ballybricker game, Dromtarry were already losing by four points to one. Not the best start to the season. The shell-shocked players stood in a circle around Murph as he punched his right fist in his hand. His usual way of emphasising every statement he made.

'Ye'll have to work that bit harder.' Smack.

'Ye'll have to get rid of the ball faster.' Smack.

'Ye'll have to stop waiting for the ball to come to ye.' Smack.

'Remember now, ye have the wind behind ye in this half.' Slightly less of a smack.

Every one of his players was listening intently, while sucking on the sliced-up oranges being passed around by Charlie Morrissey's mother. Charlie was embarrassed at the way his mum was fussing over his team-mates. Most of them were too worried about the scoreline to notice.

Through all of Murph's speech, Shaun Reedy stood off to the side with a ball in his hand and a very serious look on his face.

'Shaun, do you have anything to add?' asked Murph at the end.

'Just one thing, Murph. If you don't mind.' His accent still drew sniggers from some of the squad. 'I'd like to talk to Davey over here for a second.'

Davey McCarthy walked nervously toward him but the American was already signalling for him to follow farther down the field. Away from the crowd. Once they were out of earshot, he squatted down to talk.

'Okay Davey, what's happening with the free shots?' he asked.

'Do you mean free-kicks?' asked Davey. He was the team's free-taker from all distances.

'Yeah, yeah, I do.'

'I don't know. They just keep going that way.'

He gestured to the right where three of his first-half frees had tailed off at the last second.

Three points that would have made all the difference.

'Okay, here's what I want you to do.' Shaun Reedy was standing up now and had placed a ball on the ground in between the pair of them. 'I want you to kick this but pretend you are doing it in slow-motion.'

'Slow-motion?' Davey didn't like the sound of that. He wondered if the others were watching. It was bad enough being the tallest kid on the field without being the centre of attention during half-time too. He hoped his friends couldn't see what was going on.

'I'm not sure about this,' he said, his head down as he spoke.

'Just give it a try. Please. Just once.' The American accent was stronger than ever.

Davey shrugged his shoulders in agreement, took three slow steps back and half-heartedly began his run-up, in slow motion, as requested. As Davey reached the ball, Reedy suddenly whisked it away to the side. Then he placed his hand on Davey's head.

'Don't move. Here's the problem, Davey, you keep lifting your head at point of impact.'

'Point of…?'

'Point of impact. When you are just about to kick the ball, your eyes are already looking toward goal. They should be looking at the ball.'

'Really?'

Davey wasn't convinced. He was also worried. He could see Peter and Charlie and all the rest of them now staring downfield. He was right where he hated to be. In the spotlight. Luckily for him, the referee started to call the teams back on.

'Eyes down every time.' The American voice was the last thing he heard as he jogged towards centre-field for the throw-in. 'Just remember that.'

It was going to be hard to forget. Every time Dromtarry won a free near the Ballybricker goal in that second half, Shaun Reedy suddenly appeared on that part of the sideline.

'Davey, eyes down.'

'Davey, remember the eyes.'

'Eyes, Davey, eyes.'

Davey went red every time he heard his name delivered in that strange accent which seemed to be getting louder and louder as the half wore on. He was so embarrassed in fact that he barely noticed the advice starting to work.

His first free split the posts from all of twenty metres out. A second from closer in yielded the same result. So did a third. With a minute to go, Dromtarry had drawn level and Davey McCarthy's cheeks were no longer so red.

That was when Johnny Delaney won a loose ball out on the wing, put his head down and started soloing for goal. He'd lost one defender and was closing in on the target when another came across and pulled him down. A free. Twenty metres out. Within scoring distance for Davey.

As he placed the ball, he could hear the

familiar sound.

'Eyes, Davey, eyes.'

The American had his cap off now and was squatting behind the goal. There was no need for the extra reminder. Davey knew what was required by then. So much so that he still had his eyes on the ground when he could hear the cheers of his team-mates signalling the ball had gone sailing over the bar.

The Ballybricker goalie took a kick-out, but time was up. Dromtarry had won their first game. As they walked off the field, Peter O'Connor came running up from corner-back towards his best friend. Everybody else was congratulating him on the fantastic free-taking. But Peter had only one thing on his mind.

'What did that American say to you?'

CHAPTER FIVE

On Monday, it was too wet to go out in the schoolyard during lunchtime so Peter and Davey just sat on a window sill, talking about the game. The exact same conversation they had outside Mass the day before. The exact same conversation they had on the way to class that morning.

'It was like magic,' said Peter.

'I know,' replied Davey. 'He just looked at me kicking and knew what I needed to do.'

'He won the game for us.'

'Eh?'

'Well you know, he helped you win the game for us.'

'That's better.'

They both laughed at that. Davey was the least egotistical kid on the whole team. He never looked for praise.

'I'm going to ask him for tips about my

game.' Peter was determined to discover if the new coach could improve him too.

'I'm not sure if he knows anything about corner-backs.'

'He's bound to. Maybe he can make me faster or something?'

They were sitting in the same spot they always sat when it rained. The only part of the window sill in the upstairs classroom that offered a view of the Dromtarry pitch down the road. Not the whole pitch. Just one half and the goalmouth where the water always gathered in the largest puddle.

Peter was tracing his name in the condensation on the glass when he suddenly started wiping it furiously to get a better view.

'Hang on a sec …' he said, now using his sleeve to rub the window clear.

'Is that what I think … I don't believe this … Is it …'

'It is,' said Davey. He was standing now too. The right sleeve of his jumper already soaking wet from clearing his own patch of glass. 'It's him alright.'

They could see Shaun Reedy with a bag of balls slung over his shoulder, walking in the rain. They knew instantly he was heading towards the pitch.

'He's not going to train, is he?' asked Davey.

'We'll soon see,' said his best friend.

They tracked his every move the rest of the way until, finally, he strolled inside the gate, and started to take off his tracksuit.

'He's not togging out in this rain?' they both asked each other.

It was lashing down. Even from nearly half a mile way, they could see bubbles being made by the larger drops of rain hitting the puddle in the penalty area. Still, the American was slowly preparing some elaborate exercise. It involved ten rugby-shaped balls being placed in a straight line stretching from the 13 metre line out to halfway.

'What's he doing now?'

Peter had no time to answer Davey's question because Shaun Reedy had already begun his own personal work-out. He was trying to kick each ball through the goalposts and they watched him succeed with the first nine.

That left just one more. The ball was on the line in the centre of the field where the throw-in takes place.

'That's seventy metres or something isn't it?' asked Peter.

'At least,' said Davey.

'He'll never do it.'

'He just made one from a few feet closer.'

As they spoke, Shaun Reedy stood completely still in the middle of the field for just a second. Then, he took three quick steps and – his eyes always looking down of course – kicked a beauty. High and straight. Just like the other nine, it split the posts perfectly and made his long-distance fans even more amazed than before.

'It's like he has a cannon for a foot.'

'I've never seen anything like it.'

'I don't think even Mickey Walsh ever made one from that far.'

Mickey Walsh was the best player in the club. He played centre-field on the Cork senior team and was Peter and Davey's hero. Well, he had been until they witnessed Shaun Reedy's display.

'What are ye two up to?'

Their lunchtime show was suddenly interrupted by their teacher Mr Nelligan.

'We're just watching our American coach taking frees.'

'Your American coach?'

'Yeah, Murph brought him in. He's called Shaun Reedy.'

Peter delivered the name with the best accent he could muster, an accent the product of too many years watching Nickelodeon and the Disney Channel. It was so impressive even Mr Nelligan smiled.

'Can we keep watching?' pleaded Peter as the ten balls were placed back in a row out on the field.

'No, lunch is finished. Get back to your desks lads, the show is over.'

For them, the show was over but the talking would continue.

'Where did he learn to kick like that?' Davey was whispering as Mr Nelligan wrote sums on the board.

'With such a short run-up too,' said Peter, his left hand over his mouth to further reduce the volume.

'I don't know, but there's definitely more to this guy than Murph is telling us.'

CHAPTER SIX

'**W**hat's he doing?' asked Peter.
'I'm not sure,' replied Davey. 'I think it's some sort of gymnastics.'

'It looks like yoga to me.'

'What do you know about yoga?' Davey didn't believe Peter even knew what the word meant.

'My mum does it in the club hall every Tuesday night. She has a mat just like that one.'

Peter was pointing through a large window to where Shaun Reedy was sitting cross-legged on a mat in an otherwise empty room. The two boys were perched on sturdy branches halfway up a large oak tree in the garden. Well, it used to be a garden. Everything was so overgrown it had taken them a good half an hour to cut their way through the bramble and weeds.

The spying mission had been Peter's idea.

Once he'd overheard his parents talking at dinner about the American fella staying up at the old, grey house on Baker's Lane he'd began planning the whole operation. Once he learned Friday was a half-day from school, he declared that afternoon to be the perfect time for the mission.

'He hasn't moved for a very long time,' said Davey anxiously.

'I think that's the way it's supposed to be,' said Peter, trying to sound like he knew something about yoga.

'No, I mean he hasn't budged. He's just sitting there with his eyes closed. That can't be good.' His concerned voice was soon matched by his friend's.

'Do you think he's okay?'

'I'm not sure,' said Davey, now using the anxious voice of a boy already beginning to regret this whole thing. Cork City had just taken an unlikely early lead against Barcelona on FIFA 09 when Peter had rung the doorbell.

Davey was starting to wish he'd stayed home with his beloved Nintendo Nunchuk in his hand.

'Let me see.' Peter was leaning out over the branch now to get a better look.

'His eyes are completely shut,' said Davey.

'Don't worry about that. That's how my mum does it.'

'Does she sit still for that long?'

Peter didn't answer because he was already moving out along the branch to take a closer look.

'I should have brought my Dad's racing binoculars,' was all he said.

'Binoculars? It's bad enough that you have a torch in your jacket,' said Davey, now getting seriously worried about where this whole business was headed.

'You always have to have a torch when you do stuff like this,' whispered Peter. 'Even in the middle of the afternoon?' asked his friend.

Peter didn't reply to that one and Davey

continued to grow more concerned. Not least because the branch wobbled a little bit more the farther Peter edged out along it. He was about to warn his friend to be careful when suddenly they had something much more important to worry about.

Through the window, they watched Shaun Reedy fall to the floor, his right hand clutching at his chest and his mouth open as if he was screaming in pain. The boys looked at each other. Stunned.

'I, I … I think he's having a heart attack,' said Peter. 'I saw one once on *Home and Away*.'

Davey didn't respond because without saying anything else, the pair of them jumped off the tree so fast they almost became tangled up in each other when they hit the ground.

It must have been seven feet all the way down. But the mixture of excitement and fear surging through their bodies meant they felt no pain. They just scrambled to their feet and ran towards the house. They hurdled old branches that lay in their path, ignored the threat of over-sized nettles.

'We don't even know where the phone is to call an ambulance,' shouted Davey breathlessly as they sprinted.

'This is why I keep telling my mum I need a mobile phone,' rasped Peter.

Within seconds, they were pushing in the enormous front door. It only opened halfway before getting stuck but that was enough. Then they began trying to figure out which door led to the room where Shaun Reedy lay.

'We're coming!' shouted Peter. 'Hang in there.' As he spoke, he opened a door halfway down the hall. An empty closet! Davey had already moved ahead. The first door he tried was stuck. He put his shoulder to it but it was no good.

They turned the corner at the bottom of the stairs together. To their right, a red door was ajar and opened into a room full of light. Bingo! This had to be it. They ran towards it with Peter, of course, shouting as they did.

'You look for the phone and I'll–'

Peter never finished his sentence because the pair of them stopped dead in their tracks just inside the door. They rubbed their eyes with disbelief. They gulped. And they wondered what could possibly have happened.

CHAPTER SEVEN

The mat lay empty on the floor. The rest of the room was also completely bare. Not a stick of furniture. Just that empty mat where thirty seconds or so before, they'd seen Shaun Reedy having what looked like a heart attack. Hadn't they?

'Wha… wha… what happened?' asked Peter. He only ever stuttered when he was nervous or scared. Right now, he was both.

'I don't know,' replied Davey. He was trying to remain calm, but both of them were too afraid to move. They just kept staring at the long stretch of green foam hoping Shaun Reedy might suddenly materialise on it.

'Should we touch it?' asked Peter.

'No way,' said Davey.

'Well, what then?'

Suddenly Peter was no longer the leader of the expedition. He was now desperate for

Davey to make a decision about their next move.

'I think we should just get out of here,' said Davey.

'What if he's dead?'

'If he was dead, he would still be there on the mat.'

Davey was pointing at it and his hand was shaking just a little. This was way more than they bargained for when they'd set off up the hill earlier that afternoon.

Without another word, they backed slowly through the door. In the hallway, they kept walking backwards slowly until they reached the corner by the stairs. Then, as if each knew what the other was thinking, they suddenly started to run toward and through the front door.

They were high-tailing it back through the garden when suddenly, they heard a voice from above.

'You guys looking for something?'

In their desperation to stop, they both tripped and fell over into a pile of dead branches. When they picked themselves up and turned around, they saw Shaun Reedy. He had his legs crossed again but this time he was sitting in the very tree from which they'd spied on him earlier. He was also wearing an enormous grin. And waving a torch.

'I think you dropped this, Petey,' he said.

'It's Peter actually.' Peter spoke in the voice he used when his parents made him clean up his room.

'Peter, then. It's still yours though, right?' At the end of the question, Shaun Reedy swung down from the tree. He made one of those impressive landings the boys had only ever seen gymnasts do at the Olympics on television.

'What are you guys exactly doing here today?'

They shrugged their shoulders as if he was the school principal and they were in his office.

He didn't appear to notice because he was still talking.

'I watched you trashing around in the bushes out here. You guys are lucky you didn't get badly stung. Tough nettles around these parts, you know? What was with the spying on me from up in the tree?'

No answers. Just embarrassed looks and more shrugging.

'You guys were like the Hardy Boys out here.' Shaun Reedy was smiling at their discomfort.

'The wrestlers?' asked Peter, unable to keep silent any longer.

'Wrestlers? I mean the detectives. You know, the books, the old television series?'

They didn't.

'The only Hardy Boys we know are on the WWE,' said Davey.

At this, Shaun Reedy laughed even harder than before. So much so that Davey wondered whether he was gently mocking them like the school principal Mr Lynch sometimes did.

'A different set of Hardy Boys, but anyway, why didn't you just knock on the door and call in?'

'Well, you know, we don't really know you that well,' said Davey.

'Fair enough, but you're here now. How can I help you?'

The question stumped them. They hadn't come up to the house to talk to him. They were just being nosey and wanted to look around. Now, he was gesturing for them to sit down on the window sill to chat. That wasn't part of Peter's plan, but fortunately he soon remembered there were plenty of things he wanted to know. So many indeed that he rattled them all off at once.

'Where are you from in America? Why did you come here? Do you own this house? How do you know Murph? Did you ever play Gaelic? Did you even know what it is?'

'Woah, hold your horses there, man. That's a

lot of questions at once. I grew up outside New York. I do own this house because it was once my Dad's. I know Murph because he and my Dad played on the Dromtarry minor team of 1963, the one that won the county.'

His audience began nodding their heads. Now it was all starting to make sense.

'I played Gaelic football for a couple of weeks when I came here one summer with my Dad.'

'Were you any good?' Peter continued the interviewing.

'No, all the kids laughed at me because I couldn't kick the ball straight.'

'What has you here now?' Peter was quizzing him like the detective he wanted to be when he grew up.

'Eh, I just, um, I just, eh, wanted to see the house after all these years.' There was hesitation in the answer, but the two boys didn't notice.

'Will you be staying long?' Davey at last

offered a question of his own.

'That I don't know. All I do know is that I'll be at the match Sunday morning.'

He clapped his hands together loudly then as if signalling it was time for them to leave. Peter and Davey got up and noticed he had his right hand raised. They knew enough about America to guess what to do next.

Two high-fives later, they were leaving the old Reedy house by the dirt path road rather than through the overgrown fields.

CHAPTER EIGHT

From the moment the ball left the Car-rigowen centre-fielder's foot, Peter could see it heading his way. He knew from the flight it was going to bounce before reaching him so he timed his run perfectly. He caught it just as it bounced back up off the ground, his fingers wide apart to grab and bring it into his chest. A body catch. Just like Murph had been teaching them for weeks.

'Bring it into your chest and hug it like it's your baby brother,' he'd told them, at least a thousand times.

Peter headed off on a solo run then, moving diagonally to get away from the corner-forward who was in hot pursuit. In between flicking it from toe-to-hand, he was trying to look up. Another cardinal rule drilled into them by Murph, a man who spent what seemed like hours trying to remind them the game was all about passing.

'Seek and ye shall find. Seek and ye shall find'. That was Murph's motto, but the boys could have sworn they'd heard it somewhere before too.

As Peter moved forward, the strangest thing occurred to him. For the first time in his brief football career, he wasn't panicked with the ball in his hand. Usually, he got so excited in possession that he just booted it forward and hoped for the best. This was different.

He knew Dromtarry were two points down and that time was almost up. He knew his job was to get the ball downfield as quickly as possible. Yet, he felt like he was in control. Maybe it was the wonderful catch he'd made but something had certainly given him confidence.

Never mind that it seemed the entire Dromtarry team was calling for the pass. Or that Carrigowen players were converging on him from all angles. He felt in no hurry at all until a familiar figure came sprinting into his line of sight. Off to the left, through all the bodies, he could see Davey moving across, his right arm outstretched. Available for a pass. Just like he always seemed to be.

Without even thinking, Peter kicked a perfectly-weighted ball. He didn't aim directly for him. He'd been taught better than that. Murph's laws again of course. He aimed the kick so it bounced five metres ahead of Davey in the direction in which his best friend was running.

As was normal at big moments, Davey did everything right, catching it easily on the hop and clutching it to his chest. Another perfect body catch. Murph would be pleased.

Davey was tall, and his long strides gave him a huge advantage over other players. Sometimes, it seemed like his feet barely touched the ground as he soloed over the forty-five and towards goal. Just like Peter, he now heard his name being shrieked all over the pitch. The shouts didn't matter. He knew what he wanted to do. He was looking for Johnny Delaney in the corner.

On his third toe-to-hand, he glanced up and saw Johnny make his move, waving two hands above his curly head like a castaway on a deserted island trying to attract the attention of a passing plane. Seconds later, Davey had delivered a delightful pass and Johnny was in possession, steaming towards goal. He dummied one defender and as the keeper advanced, Johnny flicked the most delightful lob over his head. It bounced once on the line then rippled the net. Nobody else on the team could have done it. Maybe nobody else in the whole league.

Few could match Johnny's technique for celebrations too. He pulled the number 15 shirt clean over his head and ran towards the side-line waving it in the air with his right hand. Within seconds he disappeared beneath a pile of team-mates. Even Peter made the run all the way up the field to join in. By the time he arrived, the referee was already telling them to cop on and get on with the game.

There was nothing to get on with. Less than two minutes remained before the ref blew his whistle to signal another Dromtarry win. Except this time not everybody was thrilled. Murph and Shaun Reedy stood side by side watching the celebrations with strangely grim faces. They weren't even smiling. Soon, their players found out why.

'That was the most embarrassing thing I've ever seen in forty-odd years with this club,' said Murph. He was speaking in his serious voice, the one he used when kids wouldn't behave during training or on the bus going to or from matches. All around the dressing-room, eyes were suddenly staring at the floor.

'Johnny, that was a wonderful goal but all that rubbish that came after it,' said Murph, still glowering at them. 'There's no need for that. No place for it at all. And the rest of ye had no business getting involved either. That might be how soccer players do it on the telly, but that's not going to wash out here. Never has. Never will.'

Shaun Reedy was by his side and he chipped in too.

'Guys, awesome win, awesome goal, but that stuff, well, you know, we have a saying in America. When you score, you gotta act like you been there before.'

There was silence then for a few seconds. A few seconds too long for Peter.

'What does he mean?' he said, whispering to Davey, his hand over his mouth to keep his voice down. Not the sort of question he wanted anybody else to hear.

'I don't know,' said his best friend, 'but it doesn't seem like he's pleased with us either.'

CHAPTER NINE

On Monday morning, Peter's mother gave him money to buy his lunch in the Spar on the way to school. A rare treat. Usually, that only happened on Fridays.

'We won't be making a habit of it,' she warned as he stood in the hallway for his usual final inspection. 'It's just I know you are a bit down in the dumps after yesterday.'

She was right. Peter wasn't too happy. He couldn't believe winning a game could feel this strange. He'd loved celebrating Johnny's goal. Almost as much as he'd loved the goal itself. Now, the grown-ups had made him and his team-mates feel stupid about it.

Davey was waiting at the corner. Same as every day. He was wearing his usual Monday morning glum face too, except today it was slightly worse. No need to ask. The goal incident.

'I can't believe how annoyed they all were,' said Davey.

'I know, I know,' agreed Peter.

Peter was already walking ahead at pace.

'Why are you in such a hurry?' Davey was puzzled, He was normally the one obsessed with getting to school on time.

'I have to buy my lunch at the Spar.'

'Oh, great.' Stopping on the way to school was never Davey's favourite thing. Now he had to worry about being late too.

'What's wrong with that?' asked Peter.

'What if we meet Shaun Reedy in there?' asked Davey. 'He goes in there nearly every morning.'

'If he's there, he's there, I have to get a roll for my lunch.'

'You won't eat all that roll.'

'I know, but I'm going to try.'

Every Friday, Peter bought a breakfast roll at the Spar for his lunch. The farthest he'd ever managed to get was two-thirds of the way through it. Each week, Mr Nelligan lectured him about the left-overs. He even held him up as a bad example when teaching about the Great Famine.

They turned onto the Main Street. No sign of the Ford Focus with the tell-tale D-reg.

'We're in the clear,' announced Peter and the pair of them sped up. Even better, the shop was completely empty when they walked in.

'The heroes of the hour,' bellowed Paudie Sweeney from behind the deli counter where he was arranging meats in the display. He made them smile. The way he always seemed to do.

'Can I have a breakfast roll please, Paudie?' asked Peter.

'In a second boy, in a second.' He spoke with the air of a man with more important business at hand. Then he crouched and disappeared from view.

'What's he doing?' wondered Davey aloud, his familiar concern about being late for the roll call now kicking in. Peter hadn't time to reply because they soon had their answer.

Paudie Sweeney was standing on top of the counter with a huge grin on his face. Before they could speak, he jumped onto the floor and began doing laps of the aisles. All the while, he was waving his white butcher's coat over his head and laughing like a lunatic.

Having barely avoided crashing into the tinned vegetables aisle on his second lap, he finally stopped moments before slamming into the magazine rack. His red face looked set to burst and he could barely get out what he was trying to say.

'Sorry … There … lads, I just felt like doing a Johnny Delaney to start the week.' He was leaning on the counter. Laughing and trying to catch his breath. 'I'm not fit enough for this kind of thing.'

Paudie looked so ridiculous as he struggled to put back on his white jacket that Davey and Peter began to laugh too. For the first time since the aftermath of the goal.

'You didn't think the celebration was a bit much, Paudie?' asked Peter nervously as he handed his money over for the gargantuan roll.

'Not at all, sure ye're only young fellas. That match was pulled out of the fire. After coming back like that, you deserved to enjoy it.'

'It's just Murph and—'

'Ah don't mind Murph. He trained your fathers and some of your fathers' fathers, but sometimes he forgets the world has changed.'

'So you weren't embarrassed about it?' asked Davey, now brightening up again at hearing Paudie's attitude to the whole business.

'Not at all, boys. In fact, I'm only sorry somebody didn't get a photograph of ye all piled on top of one another. It would have made a great shot for the wall of the clubhouse.'

'Thanks Paudie.' They both said it together because they were thanking him for way more than the breakfast roll. Suddenly, the fact they'd won their second game of the season seemed way more important than what happened afterwards.

'One more thing, lads,' said Paudie as they were almost out the door. 'No need to tell anybody what you saw in here this morning.'

They answered the request with two very broad smiles. Maybe Monday wouldn't be so bad after all.

CHAPTER TEN

'**E**VERY HERO NEEDS A TEAM. EVERY TEAM NEEDS A HERO.'

Peter stood two feet inside the dressing-room door, read and re-read the poster. He still couldn't quite figure out what it was supposed to mean. He nudged Davey, but he wasn't so sure either.

'I *think* I know what it means,' said Davey uncertainly. 'But what about that one?'

He was pointing to the other wall. They'd been so busy trying to figure out the first poster they didn't notice the dressing-room had been papered with dozens of different sentences.

A chain is only as strong as its weakest link.

There is no 'I' in team.

Be the best that you can be.

Respect the game.

Great players are made not born.

Together we are stronger; together we are better.

These signs were everywhere. A few were blocking the windows. More were dangling from the ceiling by string. Peter and Davey had made sure to be early for the first midweek training session of the season. They'd even come straight from school with their gear in their bags. Their reward was to get the first glimpse at this.

'Who did this? What's it for? What does it all mean?' Peter was asking the questions aloud, walking around and reaching up now and again to touch some of the hanging signs. Davey was still too busy taking in the whole spectacle to even bother trying to answer. He mostly just scratched his head the way he always did when a question stumped him in class.

Finally, the other players started to trickle through the door in ones and twos. They were equally stunned. Charlie Morrissey gasped at the sight. Johnny Delaney just laughed out loud like a man who'd lost his mind. All were puzzled and wondering one thing: Who would have done this and why?

'What's got into Murph?' asked Johnny Delaney when he finally threw his gear bag into the corner after first doing a lap of the room to closely inspect each sign. He soon had his answer.

'Murph didn't do this,' said Shaun Reedy, suddenly filling up the doorway. 'I did.'

Heads nodded all around the room. Of course. They should have known. They should have guessed at least. But they didn't.

'First things first.' He was standing in the middle of them all now, with a clipboard in his hand. The kind of clipboard Mr Lynch the school principal always carried around on sports day. Immediately, Peter was wondering what he intended to do with that.

'Murph can't make it today. He's above in Cork on business and won't be back until tonight. He asked me to look after the session.'

'And what's all this about?' asked Peter,

pointing to the posters and speaking in the almost adult tone he sometimes used to get a laugh from the other kids. He succeeded. There were giggles all around the room.

'This is sports psychology. The power of positive thinking. It's about getting you in the right frame of mind. Positive visualisation'

Four sentences. Each one flew higher and higher over their heads.

He clambered up on the bench and ran his hand beneath one of the signs for effect.

'There is no "I" in team,' he practically shouted.

'We know that,' said Johnny Delaney. 'We might only be in fifth class, but we can all spell "team".' Then he did just that, for extra comedic effect, 'T-e-a-m.'

There were sniggers all around.

'No, you don't get it.' Shaun Reedy had never sounded more American and less sane to them. 'It's a figure of speech. It's not about spelling. It's about *meaning*.'

From Charlie Morrissey in his favourite corner near the door to Peter and Davey sitting by the entrance to showers, the boys' faces all wore the same puzzled looks.

'Well, maybe you'll get it eventually.' Shaun Reedy had jumped down from the bench. He looked smaller than usual and a little bit disappointed. 'I'll leave these up for a while anyway.'

The team started to get togged out in near silence. The first time that happened ever. Well, near silence.

'I feel sorry for the guy,' whispered Davey to Peter.

I know,' said Peter. 'He's just standing there. He doesn't know what to do.'

Without even running the idea past his best friend, Davey stood up and shocked the room.

'I'm ready to go,' he said, picking an O'Neill's football out of the net bag and bouncing it. 'I want to be the best that I can be.' Then he put his hand out to high-five Shaun Reedy on his way out the door to train.

Maybe it was the smile that simple gesture brought to the American's face. Perhaps it was just copying Davey because he was the best player on the team. But the funny thing is everybody else decided to do exactly the same thing. They stood up one by one, and declared 'I want to be the best that I can be', and then delivered the high-five.

Shaun Reedy was the last one out of the dressing-room, but he was probably the most excited of all.

CHAPTER ELEVEN

'This is just like training with Murph,' said Peter. He was in a group of players standing behind the goalposts getting ready to solo around some cones.

It was exactly like training with Murph. They did the blocking drill where one player is on his knees with his arms outstretched. They practised kick-passes. They even had a very brief game of backs and forwards.

'Except he's a lot louder than Murph,' said Davey. 'And he's got a clipboard in his hands. I'd love to ask him what that's for.'

'He's probably giving us all marks out of a hundred,' said Peter, tapping the ball from toe to hand.

'Do you really think so?' asked Charlie Morrissey.

'No, it's just all American coaches have to have clipboards,' said Peter in a voice that suggested he knew more about the subject.

'Why?' asked his disbelieving team-mates.

'Have you ever seen Madden '09?' asked Peter, by way of explanation. 'They all have them. Every coach in the league.'

If it existed in a video game then it had to be true. Peter smiled. He knew his pals were impressed by this explanation.

'Okay guys!' Shaun Reedy had sprinted over to them so fast nobody had seen or heard him coming. They all looked at each other afraid he'd overheard their little chat.

'Everybody gather around me and take a knee.' Nobody knew what that meant until he knelt down on one knee and gestured for them to do likewise. They all felt a little weird doing it, but nobody was brave enough to speak up and complain.

'Okay, what's the worst thing about the weather here?' asked Shaun Reedy.

'The rain,' said Johnny Delaney. Always first off the mark.

'Exactly,' said Shaun Reedy, clapping his hands in delight at the answer. 'How many matches do you have to play in the rain?'

'Too many of them,' Everybody seemed to answer that one together.

'Well, where I grew up we didn't have rain that much, and you want to know a secret?'

The question and answering stuff started to remind Davey of the time his mother had brought him and Peter up to Cork for the Christmas pantomime when they were seven. Especially when the rest of the team responded together with a resounding, 'Yesssss!'

'When I was your age, if it rained, we weren't allowed to play.'

Every one of them started to laugh. Johnny Delaney found it so funny he could no longer balance on one knee and fell to the ground. Which caused more laughter.

'I guess our parents thought we were kind of soft,' said Shaun Reedy. 'They were afraid we'd melt.'

The Dromtarry Under-11s were loving every minute of this and it was only going to get better.

'Here's a little drill I call fishing for glory. Please turn around.'

They were now facing the area behind one of the goals where the pitch was so waterlogged from the heavy rain that a little pond had formed. He had cones already arranged so they formed an orderly queue.

'Okay, here's what we are going to do. I'm going to throw the ball in the air over the water and your job is to retrieve it wherever it lands. I don't care if you catch it in the air or not. Just get it wherever it lands.'

Johnny Delaney was first. A good choice. He could catch the ball no matter what position he was in, on the ground or in the air. He went splashing through the water, plucked the O'Neill's from the air and then fell right down until he was wet up to his neck.

Everybody cheered. Then they each

followed suit. Some slid into the water. More tried a sort of surfing they'd seen on television shows. All were sopping wet and smiling by the time they reached the other side with the ball in their hands.

'Do you want to go again?' asked Shaun Reedy to the group of drowned rats now standing before him with stupid grins on their faces.

'Yesss!!'

Off they went one more time. Each one never happier than when sliding through water in pursuit of a greasy and elusive ball. When it was over they started to walk back towards him, their boots squelching beneath them. Then, they looked up and collectively gasped.

Shaun Reedy had started to sprint at full speed towards the pond. He had his arms out wide the way kids do when playing airplanes in the schoolyard at lunchtime.

'I don't believe it,' said Davey.

'I do,' said Peter with laughter in his voice.

As he spoke, this crazed American threw

himself head first across the water and came skimming to a halt a few feet later. His entire body was nearly submerged. The entire squad was so stunned they didn't even have time to cheer.

When Shaun Reedy finally stood up, his face was caked in mud. He looked like a sea monster. Everybody applauded then. Even some of the parents, by now arriving in the carpark to pick up their sons, were cheering from behind the fence. Nobody could ever remember training ending like this. Murph would never have done that.

As they walked from the field, Peter noticed the clipboard had been left lying against the fence. Picking it up to bring it to Shaun Reedy, he couldn't resist having a sneaky look first. He quickly turned it over to the front page where three large letters had been written in marker.

Together, they spelt 'F-U-N'.

CHAPTER TWELVE

Peter and Davey were sitting at the table in the McCarthy's kitchen. Davey's mum had given them the use of her work laptop. And had issued several warnings about them not spilling anything on it.

'Go to Google,' said Peter.

'I've used a computer before, you know,' said Davey. He was in charge of typing because it was his house, but the plan was Peter's idea. As usual.

He wanted to Google Shaun Reedy to find out more about him. He'd seen detectives do it on a television programme one night. A programme his mother had given out to him for watching while she was on the phone in the other room.

Davey was against this whole thing. He felt it was snooping and that wasn't good. Especially since the American had turned training into such great fun. And helped him so much in the game against Ballybricker. Not to mention that he'd been so nice to them both that day up at his house. Still, Peter somehow convinced him it was a good idea.

'This will help us just get a little background on the man,' said Peter. Davey rolled his eyes, recognising this word as something else his friend had picked up from the telly. He keyed in the name anyway and pressed enter.

'Three hundred thousand results!' shouted Peter, jumping out of his chair with excitement. 'Either there are a lot of Shaun Reedys in the world or this guy is very famous for something.'

Mrs McCarthy had loomed back into view. Attracted by the noise of Peter no doubt.

'Why don't you go to Wikipedia, Davey?' she suggested. 'It has mistakes in it but usually the basic facts will give you some idea about a person.'

One move of the mouse later, there it was, laid out in black and blue words on the computer screen. The explanation for exactly why

Shaun Reedy was living in Dromtarry.

'From Wikipedia, the free encyclopedia:

Shaun Buachaill Reedy (born January 17, 1981) in Wading River, New York, is an American football placekicker with the New York Giants of the NFL. Most famous for missing a field goal in the final seconds of the Super Bowl that cost his team the game. Went into hiding immediately afterwards. Unconfirmed reports allege he's currently travelling in Asia...'

There was silence. Finally, Davey spoke up.

'What does all this mean, Mum?'

'Um,' said his mother, rather nervously, 'it means, well I think it means your friend is basically taking a break over here because of what happened in that match. Obviously, it didn't go well for him.'

'Why does it say he's in Asia then?'

'I told you, sometimes Wikipedia isn't 100 per cent accurate.'

'We can see it on YouTube.' Peter was shouting again because he'd had a brainwave 'The field goal thing, I mean. If that part is true, it's bound to be on YouTube'

He was practically jumping around the room in anticipation of what might come next.

'Yes, you probably can,' said Mrs McCarthy. She sounded much less enthusiastic about the whole project now that the pair of them had uncovered something so serious.

Peter was already leaning over the keyboard, urging Davey to click and type faster. There was no need to hurry though because, within seconds, it was there before their very eyes, complete with live commentary.

'... *with three seconds remaining in the Super Bowl, it falls to the New York Giants' place-kicker Shaun Reedy.*'

They couldn't see his face. Just a guy in an enormous helmet lining up to kick a ball.

'*He's sprinting on to the field now and all of America is watching. If he can convert this forty-two yard field goal, he will win his team the world championship.*'

The stadium was an enormous bowl shape just like the ones on Madden '09. It was completely packed.

'Calm as you like, he's swinging that trusty right foot back and forth as he warms up ... He looks very composed and why wouldn't he be? He hasn't missed a field goal from any distance in over a year...'

They still couldn't see his face but they recognised the warm-up routine. That was exactly the kind of stuff he did the day they watched him from the school window, kicking all those balls in the rain.

The ball is snapped ... He's kicked it ... It has the height ... It looks good ... but no, it's gone left and wide. A matter of inches. But wide ...oh so wide ...

It had looked good. Then, it just trailed off at the last second. Peter and Davey's eyes were also wide as they stared at the screen.

Reedy has collapsed on the field ...Not a single team-mate has even walked to console him ... He's just lying there with his face in his hands ... wondering where it all went wrong.

They must have watched it a dozen times in a row. Each time they winced a little bit more. It was horrible. The way he ended up on the grass with his head in his hands. The way none of his team-mates went to console him, the way Cork players did to each other whenever they lost to Kerry.

'What are we going to do now?' asked Davey. The look on his friend's face reminded Peter he hadn't wanted to do this in the first place.

'We shouldn't tell anybody about this,' said Peter.

'What if somebody else finds out?'

'Then they find out. But we're not going to say anything.'

Mrs McCarthy was standing behind them now, a hand on each of their heads.

'I think it's for the best all right lads not to be telling people about this.'

They nodded in agreement. Then they turned around and watched it again. A dozen more times.

CHAPTER THIRTEEN

Davey was jogging back out to the centre of the field for a kick-out when he heard Murph calling his name. He turned and saw Shaun Reedy also had his right hand in the air beckoning him to the sideline. It was raining heavily, but he recognised the signal and he didn't like it.

'No, no, no,' he said, under his breath. Not quite loud enough for the players around him to hear.

Murph had warned them about this at the start of the year. The same way he'd be warning kids for generations. On his team, everybody who trains gets to play in the games. Other teams might do it differently. Not the Dromtarry Under-11s.

'You mightn't believe this, but the best players now aren't always the best players later. Everyone needs time to grow. That's why everybody will be substituted at some time so everybody gets to play.'

Davey started walking towards the bench. He was trying not to let his feelings show. He was trying to remember Murph's words. He hated going off though. Even if Dromtarry were leading Clonhaven by 1-7 to 0-4 with just ten minutes left.

It was only when he looked to the sideline that Davey realised Murph was right. Anthony Murray was jumping up and down, wearing the biggest smile of his life as he got ready to run on for his first substitute appearance of the season, at centre-field. Of all places.

'The job is done,' said Murph, putting his hand out to shake it as a now-smiling Davey went past.

The only problem was the job wasn't quite done. As soon as Davey went off, Clonhaven started to get the upper hand. Suddenly, the game was all being played in the Dromtarry half of the field. A point went over. Then another. A few minutes passed and then a third point. 1-7 to 0-7.

'There's only a goal in it now,' said Charlie Morrissey to Peter as he put the ball down for the kick-out.

'I think the wind and the rain are blowing against us since Davey went off,' said Peter. 'Or else it just seems that way.'

Whatever about the wind getting stronger, Dromtarry hung in there. Once or twice they got the ball back into the Clonhaven half even if they didn't score. On the bench, Davey saw Murph look at his stopwatch before telling Shaun Reedy there was only a minute left. They were bound to hang on.

Then it happened. Just as Clonhaven got ready to take a sideline ball inside the Dromtarry half, a red and white helicopter suddenly hovered into view. It was flying low enough for the players to be able to read the words Coast Guard Rescue painted underneath. It was also flying low enough for most of them to be distracted by the sight of a machine that looked like it might be blown out of the sky by a gust of wind.

Almost everybody on the field stopped looking at the ball so they could stare up at the magnificent sight, whirring around just a couple of hundred feet over their heads. Almost everybody. One Clonhaven centre-fielder saw what was happening though and seized his opportunity.

He took the kick quickly enough for one of the Clonhaven corner-forwards, probably the only other player on the field not fascinated by whirring blades either, to run into space. He collected the ball in acres of space and started pacing towards goal.

'Peter, Peter,' shouted Charlie Morrissey, quickly realising what was happening and looking desperately for somebody to stop this guy's march.

Peter sprinted as fast as he could. But the Clonhaven player was poised to shoot. His right leg was pulled back. There was nothing

left for Peter to do. Except what they'd practised in the blocking drill.

He dived full-length with his hands opened
and his arms outstretched. And he braced for
impact by closing his eyes.

Thwack. The sound of leather on skin.

Peter was so excited at the way he dived that
the ball hitting his hands so hard didn't even
hurt. He was so excited he didn't mind his face
landed in mud and was now covered in the
brown stuff too. He was so excited because he
knew that sound meant he'd stopped the shot.

Usually, it did too. Just not this time.

The ball only struck his right hand and it was
hit powerfully enough to keep going. Worse,
the deflection actually caused it to arc up into
the air and to drop just beyond Charlie's reach.

Peter only knew all this when he picked
himself up off the ground and saw Clonhaven
players celebrating. He thought the cheers
he'd heard while lying in the muck were from
his own team. Charlie didn't even have time to

kick the ball out. Dromtarry's third game of the season had ended in a draw.

Davey walked out onto the field to console his pal. Charlie Morrissey tried too. But Peter was too upset to hear anything. He blamed himself for the goal. Even though all the other backs had been too distracted by the helicopter, now long since departed up Drom mountain to rescue trapped climbers, to notice.

As the trio reached the gate out of the field, Shaun Reedy was waiting for them. He put one arm around Peter and used his hand to lift his chin up off his chest.

'Don't worry about this champ,' he said. 'You were the guy paying enough attention to even try to save the day. I don't know much about this game but I know that was a perfect block Peter. Perfect.'

'How come I didn't stop him so?' asked Peter in the angriest voice he could muster.

'Well, sometimes you do everything right

and you just get unlucky. That's the way of the game.'

Peter wiped some more muck from his face and continued walking up the hill toward the dressing-room with his head down on his chest.

CHAPTER FOURTEEN

Peter and Davey were walking home from school on Tuesday evening when they heard somebody beeping a horn really loudly. They turned to see Shaun Reedy pulling up beside them while hanging out the window of an enormous white van.

'Guys, how you doing?'

Great,' shouted Davey.

'What's with the new van?' asked Peter, always alert to the need to add to his store of information.

'I needed something bigger to do some heavy lifting.'

'Are you fixing up the house?' Peter again with the questioning.

'No, something a lot more fun than that.'

Peter's ears pricked up at the possibility of some gossip. By now, Shaun Reedy also knew he was the kind of kid who wanted to know everything that was going on in the town.

'Unfortunately, Peter, if I told you about it I'd have to kill you.'

Davey laughed. Peter didn't find that so funny. He didn't like when people mocked his curiousity. Even when it was Shaun Reedy, somebody who was fast becoming one of his favourite people in all of Dromtarry.

'If you two really want to know, meet me at the handball alley just out the Cork road in about an hour. Get your homework done first. I don't want your parents mad at me.'

The handball alley? Peter and Davey looked at each other. The handball alley hadn't been used by anybody except teenagers for years.

One bored October Saturday afternoon the previous year, Davey and Peter had thought about exploring it but it was nearly impossible to get in there. Enormous weeds and bushes were growing in the old doorway. And when they peeked through a large hole that had been smashed in the back wall, what they saw inside made them decide against going any farther.

Bicycle wheels, an upturned shopping trolley, and broken glass littered the floor. A whole lot of swear words were spray-painted around the place too. They knew then exactly why their parents always warned them off ever going in there.

'What can he be doing at the handball alley?' asked Peter.

'There's only one way to find out,' said Davey.

They ran the rest of the way home, rushed through their homework, and, exactly fifty-five minutes later were walking together to the edge of town, eagerly going toward the handball alley.

The large white van was parked on the grassy verge. There was no sign of Shaun Reedy. But that wasn't a problem because they were busy enough looking at everything else.

The weeds were gone. The gap in the wall had been filled in.

'Look at this place,' said Peter, leading the way as usual. 'I don't believe it, it actually looks like a …'

'Handball alley?' asked Shaun Reedy. He performed his usual trick of appearing from nowhere. He was wearing white overalls and carrying a still-wet paint brush.

'Exactly,' said Davey.

'Come with me guys.' He led them through the doorway into the alley, wearing the proud grin of a child about to show off his new toy.

The whole place had been cleaned up. No more glass on the ground. No more graffiti on the walls. Every weed had been removed. Even the shopping trolley was gone.

'Why did you do all this?' asked Peter

'When did you do all this?' asked Davey.

'My dad used to tell me stories about playing handball here as a kid. He even told me about the summer nights they'd have musicians playing concerts in here and the whole town would crowd in and around the place to listen.'

Peter and Davey nodded their heads. They were still in awe at what he'd done to the place to care too much about its history.

'I came in here one day the other week, climbed through the weeds and thought it would be fun to try to fix it up. So here it is.'

'You were doing this all the time? On your own?'

'Just a few hours during the day. It was fun actually. I brought Murph down this morning to help me with the targets.'

They'd been so impressed by the clean-up job that they hadn't noticed the targets painted on the main wall. Large red circles with numbers in them. Each one at different heights.

'You are standing on the shooting line.'

They looked down to see a white stripe that went right across the width of the alley.

Shaun Reedy was moving behind the line, as if readying to shoot. In fact, he was readying to shoot. From somewhere, he'd plucked an O'Neill's ball. He let fly.

'Twenty-five points!!! Not bad for an American.'

Instinctively, Davey had moved to catch the ball on its way back.

'Can I have a go?' he asked.

'Go right ahead. You guys are who this is for.'

They looked slightly bemused.

"If you fancy practicing your kicking or your fist-passing, come in here for half an hour. There's no chasing the ball, it'll come right back to you. Think of how many kicks you can take in half an hour.'

'I've seen a hurling alley set up like this in Kilturk,' said Peter.

'Kilturk!' Shaun Reedy almost spat the name out. 'Aren't those guys your big rivals?'

'Yup,' said the two boys together. 'We play them this Sunday morning.'

'Well, now might be a good time to get some kicking practice in.'

Before he'd finished speaking, Davey was already pulling back his leg to shoot.

CHAPTER FIFTEEN

The ramshackle Dromtarry club bus – everybody joked that it was even older than Murph – spluttered into the carpark of Kilturk Gaels. Murph turned off the engine and stood at the top of the aisle.

'Right lads, get yourselves ready now.' He was punching his right fist in his left hand. Already. The game hadn't even started yet.

Peter and Davey were still playing Top Trumps European Football Stars. Davey was winning and hoping to save the game until later. Peter started to pack up the cards though as soon as Murph spoke, cleverly avoiding yet another defeat.

'We don't want to annoy Murph,' whispered Peter, obviously trying to avoid any accusations of cheating. 'Not today of all days.'

He slipped the cards into the side pocket of his gear bag beneath the seat. Like every other player on the bus, Peter was already togged out. And ready for action.

This was the way of it when Dromtarry played Kilturk. The traditional refusal to use the Kilturk dressing-rooms. Nobody knew exactly why they did this. Everybody just knew it had always been the way. For as long as anybody could remember. At least that's what Murph told them earlier that morning.

'This is kind of cool,' whispered Davey. He didn't want Murph to hear him chatting either.

'What?' asked Peter.

'You know, marching off the bus and straight onto the field and everything.'

'Why?'

'I don't know. It makes us look like an invading army. Like the Vikings or something.'

'They came on ships didn't they?'

'Yeah, but it's the same kind of thing.'

Peter's mind was already racing with a different scene.

'Imagine if we came up the River Guinney

on boats. Now that would be an entrance!'

The Guinney was the river dividing the two townlands. In parts, it was only a few feet wide, but still big enough to make an enormous difference. Dromtarry and Kilturk was a rivalry dating back hundreds of years. Long before there was football, there had been competition between the two places.

'I don't need to remind ye who we are playing today,' said Murph. 'The sight of that jersey should make ye all run faster and try harder.'

The bus-load of ten- and eleven-year-old boys hanging on his every word didn't need to be told this game was a little different. They already knew. They'd heard enough talk of these matches. At home. At school. Around the club. Now, at last they were meeting the dreaded Kilturk for the first time in their short lives.

'There are only seven teams in this divisional competition so that means six matches and then the top two teams meet in the final,' said Murph. 'We can't afford to lose any games, especially against this shower.'

He was walking up and down the aisle as he told them the team. Every now and again, he stopped and tousled somebody's hair after he'd just called their name.

Shaun Reedy stood at the top of the bus, his hands leaning on the roof window above him, scanning the seats like a teacher looking for giggling pupils in class. Nobody was even wearing a sly grin.

'Finally,' said Murph. 'Remember this, a Kilturk team will always have to play twice as well as a Dromtarry team to beat us. That's just the way it is.'

His players looked puzzled as they got out of their seats.

'I don't understand what that means,' said Peter.'Neither do I. Let's just go with it,' said Davey.

They were the last two to come down the steps.

'Well if it isn't Batman and Robin, let's go

guys.' The American accent urged them on as they started to jog across the gravel of the car-park toward the field.

When they reached the gate in the fence surrounding the pitch, Peter and Davey found their team-mates had come to a sudden halt in front of them. They were all standing and staring into the goal where the Kilturk players were warming up. It didn't take Peter and Davey long to figure out what their friends were looking at.

In among the green and white striped jerseys was the largest eleven-year-old boy any of them had ever seen. He looked like an adult player who'd walked into the wrong field by mistake.

'He's even taller than Davey,' said Johnny Delancy. It was true. He was *way* taller than Davey.

'He's a lot wider than Davey,' said Peter. That was true too.

'I pity whoever's marking him,' said Charlie

Morrissey. 'It'll be like marking Optimus Prime.'

Easy for a goalie to say.

'Surely he's more like Megatron,' said Shaun Reedy, who, as usual, had silently appeared next to them. 'We're the good guys here.'

Everybody laughed.

'In America we have a saying. I'm not sure if you have it here, "The bigger they are the harder they fall".'

Encouraging words. Or at least they would have been if the entire Dromtarry team hadn't watched Megatron kick a ball high and over the bar from what looked like thirty-five metres out.

'Let's hope it rains,' said Peter.

'Why?' asked Davey.

'Because if he's made of metal he might rust by half-time.'

CHAPTER SIXTEEN

It didn't rain and Megatron wasn't made of metal. He also had a real name. Well, sort of. The rest of the Kilturk players called him 'Tank' and by half-time nobody needed to explain why to the Dromtarry boys.

Tank spent the first half barging up and down the field with the ball in his hands. Any attempt to dispossess him usually ended in a Dromtarry player bouncing off his shoulders and hitting the ground. Hard.

That Kilturk only led by two points at the break was down to one simple fact. Tank was a very unselfish player but when he passed to team-mates, most of them weren't very good at shooting at all.

Nobody from Dromtarry was taking that as any great consolation however.

'He can't be under-eleven,' said Charlie Morrissey, gulping down a piece of orange delivered by his mother as he spoke.

'Have you seen his hands?' asked Johnny Delaney. 'They're like shovels.'

'There's no *way* he's the same age as us,' said Peter, with the water bottle up to his mouth. 'Can we ask the ref to check him out?'

As they spoke, Murph stood off to the side in conversation with Shaun Reedy. Eventually, they approached their players.

'Everybody relax now,' said Murph in the same calming voice he'd been using in situations like this forever. 'The game is still there for the taking.'

There was a murmur of disbelief from his squad. A murmur he recognised all too well.

'What's the score, Peter?' he asked. Murph's tone had changed. Now, he sounded much more like a teacher on a Monday morning starting the class off on sums.

'1-3 to four points,' replied Peter.

'Two points in it and a whole half ahead of us, right?' He looked around the group to see if they were getting the message. They weren't.

'But that fella is just so big and strong, he can't be our age.' This time it was Johnny Delaney leading the protests.

'First of all, the young fella is playing and if he's playing then he's your age. Second of all, lads, never mind what he can do with the ball. Think what we can do when we have it. Concentrate on our game. Not his.'

Murph was right. Kilturk weren't that good apart from when Tank had the ball. And Murph and Shaun Reedy had come up with a plan for that too.

'Davey, you are going to take him from now on,' said Murph. 'Follow him everywhere.'

'Eh, okay,' said Davey. He didn't sound too sure he was the right man for the job. But his team-mates thought this was a great idea. The thought of their best player trying to halt the Tank's progress immediately lifted everybody's spirits.

Dromtarry walked back on to the field with a

spring in their step. Shaun Reedy walked part of the way with them because he had further advice to give to Davey.

'When he's going up for the high ball, don't try and compete for the catch, just punch the ball away so he can't get it.' The American made a punching motion that was so awkward it made Davey laugh.

But Davey did exactly as he'd been told. He followed Tank everywhere and when the ball was in the air, he did his best to punch it away from him. He didn't manage it every time, but he succeeded enough to make a huge difference.

With Tank not as dominant as he'd been in the first half, Dromtarry eventually drew level before Johnny Delaney put them a point ahead with just a couple of minutes left. Maybe they could pull this one off.

'Keep punching Davey, keep punching,' shouted Shaun Reedy. He'd spent most of the previous half hour running up and down the line delivering that encouragement, his loud American accent drawing jeers from some of the Kilturk parents gathered on the bank outside the fence.

Davey kept to the plan. As the next high ball came towards himself and Tank, he clenched his right fist to be ready, kept his eyes on the ball all the way, and then he timed his jump. At least he tried to.

Unfortunately, he didn't plant his right foot properly at the beginning of his leap. That extra millisecond meant that when he did get airborne and threw his fist toward the ball, he missed it completely. Worse again, he hit his opponent flush on the back of the head.

'*Pheewwww.*'

The refereed blew his whistle and signalled a free to Kilturk.

'It was an accident,' pleaded Davey. His protest was in vain. Tank was holding his head in mock agony. Truth be told, Davey's fist had come off worse in the clash.

The referee shook his head, wagged his finger at Davey, and put the ball down thirty-five metres out, straight in front of the goal.

It was way too far for an eleven-year-old. Well, a normal eleven-year-old. Not for Tank. He took four casual steps back and one to the side, before running up and slotting it over.

As it cruised between the posts, Peter and Charlie Morrissey looked at each other and shook their heads as it went through the posts. There wasn't even time for a kick-out. Another draw and plenty more to complaint about on the way home.

'He's *not* eleven,' said Peter as they walked from the field.

'He can't be,' agreed Charlie.

'How come there are no eleven-year-olds his size in Dromtarry?' asked Davey.

'Maybe there are and you guys just haven't found them yet,' said Shaun Reedy walking directly behind them.

The American was smiling as he spoke. A

big, odd smile for somebody whose team had just squandered a last minute lead to their fiercest rivals.

CHAPTER SEVENTEEN

Peter and Davey were fist-passing a ball to each other in the schoolyard. It was the short lunch-break and they were only allowed outside because, for the first time in days, the sun had come out.

'Wouldn't it be great if it was like this all the time?' said Peter.

'I know,' replied Davey, plucking another pass from the air. 'It never stops raining here.'

'Nice catch, Davey.'

Shaun Reedy was stopped at the wall that separated the playground from the road.

'What has you up here?' asked Peter.

'Well, detective, I'm here to see if you guys can help me.'

'What do you want us to do?' they replied together.

'Who's that kid?' Shaun Reedy was pointing to a tall fair-haired boy over by one of the basketball hoops.

'That's Linas, but we call him Lenny,' said Peter, first with the answer as always.

'I'd call him Ivan Drago looking at that square jaw and the buzzcut.'

'Ivan who?'

'Ivan Drago, the guy who fought Rocky Balboa?'

'Oh, Rocky Balboa,' said Peter, now sure of the topic. 'You mean the PSP game.'

'No I mean the fifty *Rocky* movies before there was ever a video game.'

'Sorry, we just know the Rocky from the PSP.'

Shaun Reedy shook his head. Peter and Davey just laughed at his frustration.

'Anyway, Lenny there, how come he doesn't play for the team?'

'He's from Lithuania and he only moved here last year,' said Peter.

'We asked him if wanted to play in the blitz last summer but he said he couldn't because his mother was too busy,' said Davey.

'That's no reason why he shouldn't play.' Shaun Reedy was leaning over the wall now, looking like a man on the mission.

On the other side of the playground, Lenny was shooting baskets. Just like he did every chance he got. Before school. During every break. After school when he waited for his mother to pick him up.

'He never stops playing,' said Peter as all three of them now watched him dribble the ball and shoot.

'I guessed that,' said Shaun Reedy. 'Every time I pass this school he seems to be out here. Is he taller than you Davey?'

'Oh yeah, at least six inches taller.'

'He's the best basketball player in the school,' said Peter, not wanting to be left out. Even for a second.

'Can you call him over?' Before the words had left Shaun Reedy's mouth, Peter had sprinted across to deliver the message.

Shaun Reedy was laughing at the pair of them walking towards the wall. Peter almost had to jog to keep up with Lenny's enormously long strides.

'Hi there, Lenny, my name is Shaun Reedy. I'm involved in the Gaelic football club.'

'Yes, you are the American, no?'

'Yes, I am.'

'I hear kids talking of you.'

Peter and Davey's cheeks reddened. They didn't want Shaun Reedy knowing how much they talked about him in school.

'You come from America, so do you know LeBron James, the NBA basketball player, Mr Reedy? He lives in America too.'

'Um, no, I don't, not personally. I know of him of course.'

'He is my hero.'

'I suppose he is all right if you like basketball. Anyhow, would you be interested in playing some Gaelic football with Peter and Davey here?'

'I'm not sure because I never play before.' Lenny casually bounced the basketball between his legs as he stood there. Peter and Davey watched him. They were impressed, as always, with the way he handled it. Meanwhile, Shaun Reedy continued trying to sign him up.

'Well there's a lot of catching, which you're obviously very good at from the basketball and the kicking, well, we can work on that.'

Peter and Davey glanced at each other. Now they understood what was happening. Now they knew what the smile meant at the end of the Kilturk game. It was so obvious. Shaun Reedy had spotted Lenny shooting baskets in the schoolyard and knew his height would help the team. Why didn't they think of it before? In a rematch with Kilturk he could make a huge difference.

'Okay, only one problem,' said Lenny. 'My mom, she must say yes too and you have to ask her.'

'Okay, where will I find her?'

'She work all the time at Mahony's pub.'

'Okay, I'll find her there. In the meantime I want you to do something. Davey, fist-pass that ball up over his head.'

Davey arced a beautiful pass and Lenny leapt off the ground and plucked it from the air. Then he gathered it to his chest and adopted a defensive basketball stance.

'I can see that working for us,' said Peter, suddenly grinning from ear to ear.

'You guys should show him how to fist-pass right now,' said Shaun Reedy who looked like he wanted to vault the wall and join in too.

He couldn't. So Linas Gaunas's first Gaelic football lesson of his life was conducted by Peter and Davey. They stood either side of their Lithuanian class-mate and began offering advice. All the same lines they'd been hearing since they first joined Dromtarry.

'Ball in the palm of your hand.'

'Holding hand in front of the body.'

'Close other hand in a fist.'

'Eyes on the ball.'

'Hit the sweet spot. Hit it hard.'

The first pass Lenny attempted scuffed off his fist onto the ground. The second however flew like a bullet into Davey's chest ten metres away. Just then the bell for class went.

'You guys better go,' said Shaun Reedy. I have to go too. To Mahony's pub.'

The American was suddenly marching down the road like a man on a mission.

CHAPTER EIGHTEEN

A couple of minutes before training was supposed to start, Davey stuck his head out to see if it was still raining. It wasn't. And that wasn't the only weird thing.

Paudie Sweeney and a couple of other old guys were also leaning against the wall.

'What are you doing here?' asked Davey.

'I've come to watch ye train,' said Paudie.

'You never come to watch us train.'

'Ah I do, you just don't see me.'

'You're lying, Paudie, you've never ever seen us train.'

Paudie began to blush. He was slightly embarrassed.

'Well, I know ... I heard ye signed that Russian lad whose mother works in Mahony's.'

'He's not Russian, he's Lithuanian,' said Peter. He had stuck his head out the door to see who Davey was talking to. Of course, he then had to get involved too.

'Russian, Lithuanian, it's all the same, really,' said Paudie.

'It's not. They're *completely* different countries,' said Peter. His favourite subject was geography. He already knew most of the map of Europe.

'He's from Vilnius,' said Davey. He wasn't as good at geography as Peter, but he was proud of the way he pronounced the name of Lenny's hometown.

'Is that near Moscow by any chance?' asked Paudie. He was now smiling the way he always did when they came into the shop.

'It's nowhere *near* Moscow,' said Peter, proud of the fact he knew that too.

'Look lads,' said Paudie. 'I don't care where he's from. I just know he's one big, tall lad. If I had him working for me in the shop I wouldn't even need a ladder for the top shelf.'

Peter and Davey laughed. Like they always seemed to do around Paudie Sweeney.

'Who did he play for before anyway, was it Vilnius Gaels or Lithuanian Emmets?' asked the shopkeeper.

As Paudie laughed at his own joke, Lenny came striding out of the dressing-room. He was holding an O'Neill's ball in his hand that he then started to bounce like a basketball along the path that led to the field.

Paudie and the rest of the nosey parkers stared at him like they'd never seen the giant eleven-year-old before.

'I hope you explained to the lad that he can kick the thing too,' said Paudie.

Peter and Davey had explained that and more. But Lenny's first training session was still rather eventful.

Just as Shaun Reedy predicted, he had no trouble catching the ball. He even managed a couple of powerful and accurate fist-passes. However, kicking was a problem.

'I cannot do this,' said Lenny, after trying and failing for the fifth time to manage a kick-pass to

Davey during a drill.

'No, you can, you can,' said Murph, putting his arm around him.

'Is too hard for me to learn this.'

It didn't help that everybody else was stopping their own kicking drills to look at Lenny's mistakes.

'It might seem like that,' said Murph, 'but, believe me, in a few weeks you'll be just as good as these fellas.'

Murph was being optimistic. There were times when Lenny went to kick the ball that first day that his legs looked like they weren't even attached to his body. Not that anybody dared point this out. He was suffering enough.

'I want to stop now,' said Lenny. For the umpteenth time. But Shaun Reedy was good at persuading him to keep going.

'Lenny, the first time you shot a basketball at a hoop, did it go in?'

'No.'

'How many times did you try before it went

in? How long did you play before you got as good as you are now at basketball?'

Lenny didn't answer. He just nodded his head. He understood.

'Now, try not to throw the ball up in the air before you kick it. Just let it fall onto your foot.'

Finally, Lenny made contact. Not solid contact. Just enough for the ball to leave his foot and to barely reach Davey's chest ten metres away.

Everybody cheered and Lenny smiled and put his hands in the air like he'd just scored the winning goal in the All-Ireland final.

When Davey kicked the ball back, Lenny grabbed it with ease from over his head as if it was the battered orange basketball he carried everywhere with him. Then he went to kick it back.

This time, things didn't go so well. He swung his foot too fast and the ball ended up hitting his knee and bobbling away. Before he could get upset, Shaun Reedy had picked it up and handed it back.

'Slow down, Lenny, take your time. It's going to take you a while to learn this but it's going to be worth it.'

Lenny nodded and tried again. And that was the way it went that Thursday afternoon.

He kicked some. He missed more. But, in the game of backs and forwards they played he caught everything that came anywhere in his vicinity. Two-handed catches. One-handed catches. And, like the basketball player he was, he always tried to pass.

As they walked from the field when it was all over, Peter and Davey were delighted with his impact. Even more so when Shaun Reedy walked up beside them.

'Boys, we've a saying in America.'

'You seem to have a lot of sayings in America,' said Peter, smiling.

'That we do,' said Shaun Reedy. 'But remember this one from now on: You can't coach height. You can't coach height.' He strode away rubbing his hands with glee and left his audience to figure out what he said.

'What does that mean?' asked Peter

'No idea,' replied Davey. 'I think it means he thinks Lenny's going to be good.'

CHAPTER NINETEEN

Davey was lying on the couch when he spotted Peter getting out of his mother's car and running up the path. He was sprinting to try to avoid getting soaked by the rain. It didn't work.

'You're like a drowned rat,' said Davey's mother as she ushered Peter toward the living room.

'I know,' said Peter, shaking the rain off his coat.

'I hope you're not as bored as Davey?' said Mrs McCarthy.

'I think I might be,' said Peter. 'My mother told me when I was getting out of the car not to come back for hours because she's sick of me.'

Mrs McCarthy laughed. She understood what Mrs O'Connor meant. It had been raining almost constantly for the best part of two weeks. Not the usual drizzle either. This was heavier rain than most people could ever remember and everybody in Dromtarry was fed up with being stuck indoors. Adults and children. Nobody more so than Peter and Davey.

'I can't believe we can't train or play in this,' said Davey.

'I know,' said Peter. 'No matches. No training. I feel bad for Lenny. How's he ever going to get better if he can't get out on the field?'

'His first day was the last time we trained, wasn't it?'

Peter nodded his head. They were talking like Lenny's first training session was two years ago. That's how far away it all seemed to them.

'You want to play FIFA on the Wii?' asked Peter.

'I'm sick of it. I've been playing it since I got up.'

'What about Mario & Sonic at the Olympics?'

'Played that for two hours with my dad last night.'

Peter got down on the floor in front of the television and began rooting through the box containing all Davey's games.

'You won't find anything, I'm sick of them all,' said Davey, still glued to the couch.

Peter ignored him and kept looking.

'I'm so bored I did my mum's Wii Fit this morning,' said Davey. 'I was even going to try the yoga, but was afraid I'd break it.'

'What about this?' Peter was holding up Gaelic Games Football for Playstation 2.

They both laughed. Davey got a present of it for Christmas when he was eight and the pair of them spent two frustrating days of those holidays struggling with it.

'I'd forgotten all about that.'

'Do you even have the Playstation 2 hooked up anymore?'

'No it's in the cupboard there.'

'Come on, let's give it another try.'

Suddenly Davey was enthusiastic.

'I suppose it's the closest we'll come to

kicking a ball until the rain stops.'

It took Davey a while to find the box containing the Playstation 2 console. Then he thought there was a lead missing. Eventually, they had it ready to go.

'Let's play at Pairc Uí Chaoimh,' said Peter.

Within seconds they were looking at their field of dreams. They went there two years ago to cheer on the school team in Sciath na Scoil. They desperately wanted to get back there as players themselves before going on to secondary.

'I remember the stadiums were the best part of this game, I think I can actually make out where we sat that day at the finals,' said Davey.

The stadiums remained the best part of the game, because nothing else about it had improved in the meantime. Davey won the toss to be Cork, but it didn't matter much that Peter was Kerry because an hour after they began playing, the match remained scoreless.

'I've never seen a Gaelic football match like

this,' said Peter, fed up of the fact the controls didn't work quite like they were supposed to.

'This might be the worst-designed game ever,' said Davey, making as if he was going to throw his controller across the room.

'We could play next goal wins,' said Peter.

'Except there's a chance we'll never ever score.'

'I can't play anymore,' said Peter, falling to the floor like he'd been fouled. 'This is worse than watching the rain.'

Davey sat up on the edge of couch to look out the window. Outside, the rain was worse than ever. And now there were no more video games left to play either.

Then he had an idea.

'Quick, help me here, we'll have to do this quietly, but I think it'll work.'

'What?' said Peter, not sounding like he wanted to move from the carpet. He was now amusing himself by throwing the control up in the air and catching it.

'I'm making a goal here underneath the windows. We can use that round cushion as a ball.'

'What about hitting the window?'

'We can only sidefoot the ball and the goalie has to be on his knees.'

As he spoke Davey was pushing the couch back to clear more space. Then he moved his dad's armchair over into a corner and placed his mum's favourite vase in a cupboard.

'Now I see,' said Peter, impressed with the way the pitch had suddenly been laid out in front of him. 'At last a field that can't be waterlogged.'

'I think I should shoot first,' said Davey. It had been his idea after all.

'Okay, but standard penalty shoot-out rules apply. Five pennoes each and sudden death if we're level after that.'

Davey placed the round cushion on the imaginary spot. He was all set to take a kick. Then he paused.

'One more thing. No shouting in case my

mum hears and kills me for moving the furniture.'

Peter nodded. He had his arms outstretched, ready for action.

CHAPTER TWENTY

More than an hour after starting their new game, Davey and Peter were still happily playing. Davey led by twenty-five shoot-outs to twenty, but Peter was confident he could close the gap.

Then Davey's mother burst through the door, all out of breath. The game was quickly forgotten because she had a stunned look on her face that told them something was very wrong.

'We're sorry about the noise, Mum,' shouted Davey before she could even get any words out.

'Never mind the noise,' she said. 'Come quickly. There's been a landslide down the other end of town.'

'A what?' asked Peter.

'A landslide, half the mountain is after breaking away and coming down through the far end of the town.'

She was practically pushing them into the kitchen ahead of them as she spoke.

'I want the two of ye with me, because who knows what else might happen with this thing?'

She had their coats ready on the back of chairs and the car-keys in her hand.

'Your Dad called. He's down there now helping out. It'll be a miracle if nobody was hurt.'

She rushed them to the car, ignoring questions, just talking out loud as if to herself.

'We'll just go down for a look. We'll see what the damage is. Your father sounded in a right state.'

Peter and Davey just kept nodding their heads. They knew enough to stop asking her silly questions and strapped themselves into their seats. It was only a mile from the McCarthy house to the centre of town. But they couldn't even go that far.

Once they turned the corner onto Main

Street, there was a Garda roadblock. They didn't need to ask why. From half a mile away, and even through the rain and the wipers, they could see the landslide.

A giant wall of brown mud, with trees and branches poking out of it stretched from the foot of Drom mountain all the way across the town. Water was flowing down beside the car as if draining out of it. Already a JCB was struggling to push back some of the reeds and bushes drifting down the street.

'It's like something out of a movie,' said Peter

'I've never seen anything like this in a movie,' said Davey.

'We better pray nobody was in its path,' said Mrs McCarthy.

The boys were excited by the sight of something so large and odd right in front of their eyes. Davey's mother was worried about people being killed.

'Well, those are some special effects so,' said Peter.

'I wonder could we walk along it all the way to the top of the mountain,' said Davey.

'I'm more concerned about the other direction.'

'Why?'

'From here it looks like it might have ended up by the club.'

'Eh, I hope it didn't make it that far.'

'Imagine what it could do to the field,'

Mrs McCarthy just said nothing as they spoke. Her hand was over her mouth the entire time. Davey saw this and looked at Peter. They knew it was time to shut up again.

The three of them just sat there in the car and stared at the enormous wall of mud that looked like it had cut the town in half. Which it kind of had. Eventually, without saying a word, Davey's mum turned the car and drove back to the house.

In complete silence.

There, they sat in the kitchen waiting for the six o'clock news. Mrs McCarthy had both the radio and the television on in case either mentioned it.

It was the first headline on County Sound FM.

'The town of Dromtarry was hit by a massive landslide earlier this afternoon. There are no reports of any injuries as yet, but Gardaí have cordoned off much of the town to allow emergency services and locals to search for possible victims. It's believed that the incessant rains of the past two weeks caused a portion of Drom mountain to break away and to form a fifty-metre wide trail of mud, peat and water which slid down as far as the Main Street and beyond.'

Mrs McCarthy's hand was over her mouth again. The two boys just sat there, more silent than they'd ever been when in the same room together. Only when his mother went out into the hallway to make a phone call did they talk.

'It's kind of exciting, though, isn't it?' said Peter.

'I know, nothing like this ever happens

here,' said Davey.

'Imagine if they mention Dromtarry on the RTÉ news.'

'That would be brilliant.'

And that's just what happened. Davey switched on the tv and flicked to RTE 1; Dromtarry was the second item on the news, after a story about banks and the government. Davey grabbed the remote to turn it up even louder.

'Reports are just coming in of a major landslide in Cork,' said the woman on the screen. 'The town of Dromtarry at the foot of Drom mountain was hit by a fifty-metre wide trail of mud, trees and peat earlier this afternoon.'

'Mom, you missed it, they just said Dromtarry on the news,' shouted Davey. If she heard, she didn't reply.

'I think we might have a day off school over this,' said Peter.

'We would, except I think it was in the wrong direction to hit the school.'

'Look, I don't believe this.' Peter was

furiously rubbing the fog off the kitchen window. 'I actually think the rain has stopped.'

'At last,' said Davey. The two of them started jumping around the kitchen, forgetting all about the landslide. Their joy was shortlived.

Mrs McCarthy had come back and was standing in the doorway watching them. Davey could see by her face something was wrong.

'What is it, Mum?' he asked.

'I've bad news lads, I just spoke to your dad on the phone, it's ... It's ... the clubhouse and the field ... they were both destroyed by the landslide.'

CHAPTER TWENTY-ONE

Peter and Davey were standing by a metal barrier maybe fifty metres away from what used to be the Dromtarry club. They were silent again. But this time, they each had a hand over their mouths. Just like Davey's mother the previous day.

Twenty-fours had passed since Drom mountain broke apart and now the pair of them were looking at what the landslide had done to their beloved field. To their club. To their team.

'It's gone,' said Peter, inevitably speaking first.

'I know,' said Davey.

'There's no grass. There's just that, that … brown muck.'

'Look at the goalposts.' Davey pointed to the goalposts nearest to the dressing-rooms.

The mud was piled three feet high so the bottom half of the goalposts were missing.

'They look like the small soccer goals in the gym in school,' said Peter.

'Look at the dressing-rooms.' Davey was staring into the distance as he spoke.

'What dressing-rooms?' asked Peter.

The dressing-rooms had been torn apart. The roof was completely gone. Large sections of the walls too. All destroyed by the rampaging mud and waters on their way through. On their way through to destroy the field.

'I think that's the forty-five metre line by that Christmas tree thing.' Davey was nodding towards where a fir tree was standing perfectly upright. It had been ripped from the side of the mountain and somehow planted right in a spot near the centre of the pitch.

'I think we should get some lights and hang them on that,' said Shaun Reedy. As was now the norm, the American appeared from nowhere. They hadn't even heard him coming.

'Very funny,' said Peter. But he wasn't smiling. None of them were. This was no time for jokes.

'What do you think?' asked Davey, hoping the American might have something positive to say.

He didn't. They knew this because he shook his head before he even started speaking.

'This is bad guys. There's no other way to paint it. It's awful really.'

Peter and Davey didn't even look at him. Their eyes were still straight ahead, fixed on what used to be their Gaelic football club.

Shaun Reedy immediately sensed they needed to hear something a little more positive than his first effort.

'Look, I think the important thing here is that nobody was hurt in the landslide. That was a little bit of a miracle. And I think they'll have this mess cleared in no time. Look at all the heavy machinery.'

Twenty metres away to the right, a pair of yellow JCBs were slowly pushing back mounds of mud.

Peter and Davey were unimpressed by this

attempt at lifting their spirits. And their mood got suddenly worse.

'I never thought I'd see the day Dromtarry would be on the front of the paper,' said Murph, walking toward them, clutching the *Evening Echo* in his hand.

They leaned over to gawp at a photograph of the mud bursting through Main Street.

'It's weird to see the street in a picture,' said Davey. But nobody was listening to him because Murph had already started to speak again.

'It says here that an estimated 24,000 cubic metres of material was dislodged and that the landslide picked up speed and moved at 32 kilometres per hour at one stage.'

'What's 24,000 cubic metres?' asked Peter

'A helluva lotta mud,' said Shaun Reedy.

'And most of it would appear to have covered our field,' said Murph. He had tucked his paper under his arm now and was gazing across the pitch.

'When will we be able to play again, Murph?' asked Davey.

'Will we ever be able to play again?' asked Peter.

'I wish I knew,' said their manager. 'I wish I knew.'

'Is this the end for the club?' Peter almost choked as he got the question out.

'Of course it isn't, Dromtarry has been a hundred years and it'll be here a hundred more.' Murph's tone was suddenly that of an adult fed up children's questions.

'It's going to take a couple of days to sort out where we are going with matches and training and stuff. Until we get a handle on how long the field will take to get back, we won't know for sure what's happening.'

He paused then and Peter and Davey were suddenly afraid he was about to tell them season was over.

'But don't ye worry. We've only one home game left against Carraig Crokes and we can always travel to their place for that and—'

'And the final is always at a neutral venue,' said Davey, jumping in to finish Murph's sentence.

'If we make the final that is,' said Murph. He was smiling again. Much more like his usual self.

'It's going to be hard to win without somewhere to train,' said Peter.

'Aren't you guys forgetting something?' Shaun Reedy was suddenly walking around them rubbing his hands. He couldn't wait for them to answer.

'We've the handball court. We can definitely do some sessions there.'

The handball court. The mention of it was like a lightbulb being switched on over all their heads. It had barely been finished when the rains came. Now, it might just save their season.

'We can train there tomorrow after school,' said Murph. 'I'll call the rest of the lads tonight.'

'Here comes one of them now,' said Shaun Reedy.

'The fellas from RTÉ news are down there,' shouted Charlie Morrissey when he was still twenty metres away. 'There's a van and a cameraman and everything. We're all going to make faces behind them when they start filming. You're going to miss it if ye don't come down.'

Peter and Davey turned away from the club and the mud and the Christmas tree in the middle of the field. And they went in search of the chance to stick their tongues out on national television.

CHAPTER TWENTY-TWO

The first-ever Dromtarry Under-11s' training session to be held in the handball alley was a bit of a mess. Some of the players wore their boots instead of their runners. Others were too worried about whether the team would ever play again to concentrate.

And then there was the matter of space.

'I know it's crazy guys, but just bear with us,' said Shaun Reedy after what seemed like the umpteenth kid had run too fast and almost went smack into a concrete wall.

'That's easy for him to say,' said Peter, quietly to Davey. 'He's not going to get split open trying to catch the ball.'

They had started off with a drill that involved two groups of players lining up to shoot the ball off the wall, catch it, and then fist it to a teammate. Sounded simple enough. But with twenty of them running around after balls at the same time, it quickly turned into a rugby scrum.

'I'm going to have to get more bandages,' said Murph as he knelt to deal with the fifth badly scraped knee in as many minutes.

If the session was designed to lift the team's spirits after the landslide, it was doing the exact opposite.

'This is a waste of time,' said Johnny Delaney. He didn't whisper either. He never cared who heard him say anything.

'Just give it a chance,' said Davey, always trying to keep his team-mates focused. 'It might get better.'

It didn't. Eventually, Murph called a halt and gathered everybody around him in a circle.

'Okay, we're going to change this around in a second because it's obviously not ideal. Firstly though, I want to ask you a question. Who here is worried that the club is finished and there'll be no more matches?'

Every player in front of him put their hands up. Only Peter spoke though.

'My Dad says there's talk we'll have to join up with Kilturk because the pitch will never be right.'

'That's not true. Tomorrow night, there's a meeting in the church hall where we are going to start the fundraising to get the show back on the road.'

'Can we go along to it?' asked Peter.

'Well it's for your fathers and mothers really,' said Murph. 'Just be assured, there's smart men in this club who'll find us a way back.'

'But the man from RTÉ said on the news yesterday that it could be years before the field is cleared and the clubhouse rebuilt.' Peter believed if it was on television then it had to be true.

'Let me tell you this, Peter.' Murph was speaking in a voice they didn't recognise. Half like one of their parents. Half like one of their teachers. 'That will never happen. This club will come back. Like we always do. You just worry about playing football.'

The squad seemed impressed by his message. Well, they nodded their heads as if they were anyway.

'Now, we are going to split ye into two groups,' said Murph. 'All of ye on my right come outside with me to the back where we are going to practise shooting against the wall. The rest of ye stay in here with Shaun.'

Shaun Reedy was already over in the corner fidgeting with what looked like a net.

'What's that badminton net for?' asked Davey.

'This is not a badminton net,' replied the American. 'This is a volleyball net. You ever seen volleyball?'

'On Mario and Sonic,' shouted Charlie Morrissey.

Shaun Reedy smiled, but Peter was unimpressed by this latest development.

'What good is that to us?' he asked.

Shaun Reedy didn't answer. He just walked to one side of the alley and hung the net from a hook he'd hammered in there earlier. Then he stretched it across to the other side. All the players, including Peter, were suddenly impressed.

'Five on this side of the net. Five on that side of the net.'

They dutifully moved into position. Peter and Davey together of course.

'This is called High Catch volleyball,' said Shaun Reedy. 'The objective is to catch the ball after it has been fist-passed over the net into your section of the court by the opposing team.'

Davey immediately started spreading his team-mates out to cover most of their side of the court. Organising everybody as usual. Shaun Reedy continued to explain the rules.

'To score a single point you must execute a proper catch and then a proper fist-pass over the net. The first team to fifteen points wins the game.'

That got their attention. It had been so long (more than two entire weeks, practically a lifetime) since a proper match that a competitive event of any kind thrilled them. Peter was happy at the way the line-ups worked out too.

'Between you and Lenny on this team,' said Peter to Davey, 'we've the best two fellas to catch any ball.'

He was right too. Their team did win. Fifteen points to nine. By the time Davey, of course, made the clinching catch, they were all sweating and excited.

'It's almost like a real game,' said Peter.

'But it isn't,' said Davey. Just competing again for anything had made him even more worried about the club's future.

'It was fun though,' said his friend.

'It was fun. Just not as much fun.'

Shaun Reedy was listening the whole time.

'I know you guys are worried and everything. But you have to keep the faith. Keep the faith. Do you understand what that means?' He'd hit them with another one of his American phrases.

'We do,' said Peter and Davey, even

though they didn't.

'Remember now, keep the–'

'Faith,' they said, finishing the sentence with much less enthusiasm than he'd begun it.

CHAPTER TWENTY-THREE

The oldest trick in the book. Peter told his parents he was calling over to Davey's house to play video games. Davey told his parents he was calling over to Peter's. They met halfway and then sprinted around the back of the town to the church hall for the big meeting.

When they got there, the doors were closed but not locked.

'Be quiet now going in,' said Davey as Peter went to push open the large wooden door

'I know what I'm doing,' barked Peter, already halfway in.

Once inside they edged along the back wall in the same way they always saw people doing on television shows and in movies. At one stage, Davey even put his finger up to his mouth in case Peter tried to speak again.

'This is good here,' whispered Davey. They were standing beneath the stairway at the back end of the hall. In the shadows and almost hidden from view. Perfect.

'We're going to have to peek to get a proper look,' said Peter, already leaning out of their hide-out to get a better view. 'There's your dad and my dad.'

Mr O'Connor and Mr McCarthy were sitting together at the end of a row. Up on the stage, Frankie Feherty, chairman of the club, had the microphone in his hand. There were other men sitting at a table behind him but Peter and Davey didn't know their names.

'There was a problem with our insurance,' said Frankie Feherty. 'Something in the small print. Eh, apparently, the damage to the field was not covered by our policy. Something about acts of God not being covered.'

Peter and Davey didn't know exactly what that meant, but they soon found out it wasn't good. The hall erupted into shouting and roaring. Chairs were pushed back angrily. Men, and it was mostly men, were on their feet pointing their fingers at the stage.

'This doesn't look good, does it?' asked Davey.

'I know,' said Peter. He still had a huge grin on his face though. He was kind of excited to see adults making fools of themselves like this.

Even from this distance they could see the sweat teeming off Frankie Feherty's face as he repeatedly shouted the words: 'Order, Order, Order.'

'What's that about?' asked Peter.

'It must be like when Mr Nelligan shouts *ciúnas* at us in class,' replied Davey.

Except with one difference. The men in the hall weren't willing to be quiet. At least for a few more minutes. When they finally stopped shouting, Paudie Sweeney stood up in the front row.

'There's no point fighting over the type of insurance we had. We're here to sort out where we go from tonight.'

He turned to Frankie.

'Mr Chairman, does this mean we have to pay for the field to be rebuilt out of our own money?'

'Yes it does, Paudie,' replied Frankie Feherty who then put his head down as if embarrassed.

'And how much do we think that will be?'

'The first estimate is that with the damage done, and the amount of excavation required, it's going to take somewhere in the region of three quarters of a million euros.'

The hall exploded again. Peter and Davey looked at each other but had nothing to say. Peter wasn't smiling at the adults arguing any more. Davey just looked sad. They didn't know a whole lot about money. They knew enough to realise this was bad. Really bad.

'Three quarters of a million euros,' said Davey.

'We don't have that kind of money,' said Peter.

'Where could we get it?'

'Who knows? Do banks give that kind of

money to people?'

They were still whispering even though by then, with all the other noise in the hall, they could have shouted. Their conversation was taking place against the background of grown men roaring their heads off at each other.

'I think I just heard Johnny Delaney's dad swearing,' said Peter.

'I think we better get out of here soon,' said Davey, suddenly understanding why no kids were supposed to be present.

'Why? I think this is only getting started.' Peter was getting excited again at the floor show.

Eventually, the rowing simmered down again. Paudie Sweeney took to the stage and was handed the microphone by Frankie Feherty.

'We need ideas,' he said calmly. 'We need fundraisers. We need to set up a committee to talk to the banks and to Croke Park and to the Department of Sport about loans.'

'What does all that mean?' asked Davey

'It means a group of these men are going to be given the job of finding three quarters of a million euros, very quickly,' said a voice from the darkness around the corner. An American voice. Shaun Reedy had performed his usual party trick. There before they even knew it.

'Where did you come from?' asked Peter, almost shouting with fright.

'Ssshhh,' said Shaun Reedy. 'I was watching from upstairs. Didn't know if it was my place as an outsider to be at this meeting.'

'Oh,' said Peter.

'And I know you guys aren't supposed to be here.' They smiled the smile of the guilty.

'Do you think the club is finished?' asked Peter

'No, I don't.'

'How can you be so sure?'

'I just am. I just think you should probably leave now and you should remember that you all need to keep the faith.' That same phrase again.

Peter and Davey looked at each other as they slipped out the door.

'What does he mean by that?' asked Davey.

'I don't know,' replied Peter. 'And I wish I did.'

CHAPTER TWENTY-FOUR

'I wish I was a corner-forward,' said Peter.
'I wish I was a centre-fielder,' said Charlie Morrissey.

The pair of them were leaning on either side of a goalpost. Just chatting. Right in the middle of a match. Just chatting.

'I can't believe it's our first game in weeks and I haven't even had a touch yet,' said Peter.

'I know, I know,' replied Charlie. 'Looks like Davey and the rest of them are having such fun.' He nodded down the field towards where Dromtarry Under-11s were running riot.

After what seemed like forever, they'd finally got back on a field to play. It wasn't their own field. That was still a disaster zone. The pitch belonged to Carraig Crokes and the boys were so thrilled just to be out there they played out of their skins. At least the ones playing in the Crokes' half of the pitch did.

'I don't think the ball has come into our half once,' said Charlie.

'If it doesn't come down soon, I'm going to ask to be switched upfield at half-time,' said Peter.

'Murph hates that,' said Charlie.

'I don't care, I just want a touch.'

Once the whistle had gone that Saturday morning, the players had forgotten all about the club's problems. They ignored the worrying stuff they'd heard their parents whispering about at home. They just exploded onto the pitch and, inspired by Davey, in an even more unstoppable mood than usual, were three goals and three points up after the first fifteen minutes. Two goals and two points from Davey alone.

'Maybe they'll put Davey in goal to make it fair,' said Charlie.

'He'd probably be great in there too,' said Peter.

Suddenly, they saw Murph walking down

the sideline, waving his hands at them.

'Boys, will ye stop talking and concentrate?' he shouted. He must have forgotten how hard it is to get two eleven-year-olds to concentrate when nothing's happening.

'Can you not switch us up the field?' asked Peter.

'If you stop chatting, we can talk about it at half-time.'

Half-time came and Murph was as good as his word. He switched the entire back line with the forwards, he put Davey in goal and brought Lenny off the bench to play full-forward for the first time.

The Crokes players weren't thrilled to see the blonde giant striding towards them for the second half. They were even more worried when, with his first touch, he caught a ball that seemed to be going high and wide without even jumping for it. They were less concerned though when they saw what he did with it.

In his excitement, he'd forgotten everything

he'd been told. He turned and executed a perfect jump shot, palming it basketball style over the bar.

'*Phreeeeeeeeep!*'

The referee whistled and everybody on the field laughed.

'I think you were playing the wrong game there friend,' said the ref. 'This is Gaelic football. He had the ball in his hand and he made the fist-pass gesture by way of explaining further.

Lenny just nodded

'Don't worry, Lenny,' said Peter, now lurking around the square in his new role as a greedy corner forward. 'Just take your time … and give it to me.'

He muttered the last bit under his breath. It was his dream to score a goal in an actual match and he hoped if he hung around Lenny long enough he might get just that chance.

A minute later, the ball came in again. This time it bounced right in front of Lenny and appeared to be going over his head until he stretched his left hand in the air and somehow dragged it back.

'Over here! Over here! Over here!' Peter was shouting and running. He had glory on his mind.

But Lenny didn't hear a thing. He turned and swung his right boot at the ball. And missed. A fresh-air shot so awkward he actually fell to the ground as the Crokes' defender ran away upfield with the ball.

Lenny shook his head as Peter came over to check on him

'Much easier before. Is not so easy now,' said Lenny.

'Take your time, just do fist-passes for now,' said Peter.

Murph's tactic of moving his best players away from goal had made the game more even. Crokes scored four points, Dromtarry didn't manage one and most of the second-half was played in bunches around the middle of the field.

Peter spent a lot of his time waving his hands in the hope somebody somehow would hit him with a long pass. It never came. Until right at the end. With a minute on the clock, Dromtarry won a free on the 45. Johnny Delaney, now converted into a wing-back, aimed it for Lenny.

The big Lithuanian plucked it from over the heads of three Crokes' boys. And then the most amazing thing happened. He heard Peter's shouts and saw him running diagonally across the field.

With defenders flailing at him but unable to reach up that high, Lenny delivered a fist pass that landed two metres in front of where Peter was running.

Peter felt the corner-back's hand grabbing at his shirt but he was going too fast to be stopped. He gathered the ball into his chest and bounced it once.

This was it.

He could see the goalie coming out towards

him. He could see a huge gap on the far side of the goal. That's where he aimed for when he let fly.

The ball seemed to take longer than all the goals he'd ever seen scored on television or in real life. But it got there. It billowed the back of the net. And then Peter did something that surprised himself.

Every time he'd dreamed of scoring a goal, he'd always imagined some crazy celebration routine. But now that he had scored, it was different. The game was already decided. There was no need to rub it in to his opponents.

'Yesss!!!'

He said it almost silently as he ran back to his position for the kick-out. After all that had happened, what else could he do or say?

CHAPTER TWENTY-FIVE

Peter was halfway down the stairs when he heard his parents' whispers from the kitchen. He stopped to listen. He knew he wasn't supposed to but he couldn't help it. In the weeks since the landslide, there'd been so much whispering by adults. He knew that wasn't a good sign.

'I told you not to be talking about this while Peter's in the house,' said his mother.

'I'm sorry, but you brought it up,' said his father. 'You wanted to know how much money we've raised from the fundraisers.'

'No, I asked you how much the fashion show raised.'

'And I told you about three thousand euro.'

'No, you told me that and then you told me it didn't matter because between the fashion show, the parachute jump and the race night, the club still hadn't raised more than fifteen thousand euro.'

Peter was glued to the step, leaning on the banister, trying not to make the stairs creak. He could feel his heart thumping in his chest. He wasn't great at maths, but he knew fifteen thousand euro was a long way from the 750,000 euro needed to rebuild the club.

He waited for his parents to stop talking before then very loudly bounding down the stairs, pretending he'd heard nothing.

'Will you have some breakfast love?' asked his mother.

'Naw, I'll just grab this banana, I'm meeting Davey to go to training with him.'

'I'll run you over if you like,' said his father.

'I'm grand.'

He wanted to walk because he knew if he was in the same car as his dad he would have had to ask him about the money. Not just the money but what it meant for the club too.

Davey was waiting at the usual corner with a smile on his face that disappeared as quickly as

Peter opened his mouth with a news bulletin.

'Of course it's bad, it's terrible,' said Davey after hearing the full report.

'What can we do?' asked Peter.

'I don't know. We'll ask Murph.'

They walked the rest of the way to the hand-ball alley in complete silence. The first time that ever happened. When they got there – first to arrive as usual – it didn't take long for Shaun Reedy to see something was up.

'Okay, what's wrong with the dynamic duo this morning?'

'You tell him, tell him what you heard,' said Davey.

'I don't want to get in trouble,' said Peter, 'I shouldn't have been listening.'

'You don't have to tell me anything. I think I can guess though. Is it something about the clubhouse and the field and the future?'

'Yeah,' said Peter, before letting all the money talk he'd overheard come spilling out of his mouth at once.

'I guess you got a little more than you bargained for there, Peter. Sometimes there's a price to be paid for being a detective.'

Peter and Davey didn't smile at the joke. They weren't in the mood. Both were staring at the floor of the handball alley.

'You keep telling us to keep the faith,' said Peter. 'What does that mean?'

'Um, I guess it means you have to stay strong and hope something will work out in the end for the club.'

'But *what*?'

'Um, I'm not sure, but … *something*.'

'Have you any ideas?'

Shaun Reedy was scratching his head as if by doing so he might cause a few ideas to fall out of his hair.

'Look, all I know is this. There's always a way. Right now it might not look great but this club has been around for a hundred years. That makes it almost as old as my whole country.'

The pair of them laughed at that.

'Dromtarry is a very special town. My dad always told me that and now I understand what he meant.'

'But we don't have the–' Shaun Reedy cut Peter off before he could say 'money'.

'Never mind what you *don't* have. What you *do* have is spirit. And each other.'

Peter and Davey looked at each other and smiled embarrassedly.

'You two are only kids and you shouldn't be worried about this stuff. You have to leave that worrying to the adults. It's their job to worry about money. And most of them are very good at it.'

They were still smiling.

'Now everybody's going to be here in a minute so you two need to buck up your ideas. Do you want to get some kicking down before the traffic jam starts in here or what?'

Davey was already toe-tapping a ball, eyeing up the fifty-point target on the wall and about to shoot.

CHAPTER TWENTY-SIX

'**D**eath of a club?' That was the headline on the front page of the *Evening Echo*. In giant, bold letters. Next to a photograph of the landslide and the goalposts almost submerged in mud.

Peter and Davey stared at it for what seemed like ages. Almost afraid to pick it up to read the story. They had stopped in to the Spar on the way home from school to buy Cornettos. They never reached the freezer; Davey had seen the stack of newspapers right inside the door.

'Should we read it?' asked Peter.

'We'd better,' said Davey, already stooping to pick up one of the papers.

He placed it flat on a shelf full of biscuits so they could read it together.

'Speculation is growing that Dromtarry Gaelic football club may be forced out of existence following the damage done to its premises by the Drom

mountain landslide. With 750,000 euro required to fund the redevelopment, club officers are struggling to come up with the money to even start the—'

That was as far as they got in the story before Paudie Sweeney leaned in and whisked the paper away from before their eyes.

'Boys, ye've no business reading that.'

'We do so,' said Peter.

'Yeah,' said Davey. 'We saw the headline.'

'Never mind the headline! These papers can't be trusted. You know how reporters are these days, just making stuff up.'

'We know the story is true, now can we please have it back?

'You certainly cannot. First of all, this isn't a library you know, it's a shop. You have to buy it before you read it.'

'Don't make us buy it,' said Peter.

'We just came in to get ice cream,' said Davey.

'Well I hope you have enough for ice cream and the papers. No free reads here.'

They were smiling at him. Waiting for him to smile back. The way he always did when messing with them. But this time Paudie didn't smile at all. Instead he turned away and began scooping up the rest of the papers from the rack and taking them behind the counter.

'What are you doing?' asked Peter.

'I'm putting these away,' said Paudie. 'They're not for sale anymore. I won't sell any paper full of lies.'

He'd retreated behind the counter where the pile of papers was now dumped on the floor by his feet.

'Paudie, we know the story, you know,' said Davey.

'What story?'

'About the money. We might be kids, but we're not fools.'

'Yeah,' said Peter, just wanting to have his say too.

'Well, only a fool would believe what he reads in the paper. I hope they taught ye that up in the school.'

Peter and Davey were leaning on the counter. They were staring up at him but their smiles were gone. Now they were looking at him with the pathetic eyes of puppy dogs wanting bones.

'Don't be looking at me like that,' said Paudie, pretending to be busy at the cash register. 'Do ye want your ice creams or not?'

'We're not that hungry any more,' said Davey.

'Yeah, somebody ruined our appetite,' said Peter.

'Hey, none of this is my fault,' said Paudie.

'We know that but we just want to know the whole story,' said Peter.

Paudie was pacing up and down behind the counter now, running his hands through his hair.

'Boys, ye know the club is in a spot of bother … Sure everybody knows that. But this stuff about the club going out of existence. Well that's just rubbish.'

'Why is it in the paper so?'

'Didn't I tell you about journalists? Sure I had one of them on the phone here to me the other morning, pure chancers. Now tell me how are ye fixed for the game against Newtown Rangers? Win that and you're through to the final, right?'

He was trying to distract them. Very obviously trying to distract them. They knew it too.

'It wouldn't be on the front page if it wasn't true, Paudie.' said Peter.

'What about Lenny? He's working out well for ye. Set you up nice for the goal against the Crokes there, Peter.'

'Is it true or not?' asked Davey.

'The way things are going now, it's Kilturk ye'll be playing in the final too. What a game that would be. A rematch and all.' He was still trying his best to ignore them.

'How much more money does the club need?'

'I hope you are practising your frees Davey.'

'We thought *you* at least might tell us the truth,' said Davey.

Paudie came out from behind the counter. He walked straight past them to the freezer from where he plucked two Cornettos.

'Here you go now lads,' He was holding the ice creams out one in each hand. They took them because he was smiling again now.

'We're going to find out anyway Paudie,' said Peter.

It didn't matter what they said. He was still pretending not to hear a word.

'Away with ye now and enjoy the bit of sun while it's here. Nothing at all to worry about.'

They were too smart to be fooled though.

'Things must be really bad,' said Davey as they walked down the street devouring their Cornettos.

'Why?' asked Peter.

'He didn't even charge us for the ice cream!'

CHAPTER TWENTY-SEVEN

'**W**in this one and ye are in the final against Kilturk,' said Murph to the players gathered in a circle around him.

He was punching his right fist in the palm of his left hand, standing in the middle of the field, seconds before the throw-in against Newtown Rangers.

'Win and you're in!' shouted Shaun Reedy who sounded more excited than ever before. 'Win and you're in!'

It wasn't going to be as simple as that. Newtown were good. Very good. And they had something to play for too. A win for them would also be good enough to punch their ticket to the final.

The game was close. All the way.

Having swapped the lead throughout, the two sides were level with just a minute to play.

Newtown laid siege to the Dromtarry

goalmouth for what seemed like an age. One rocket of a shot came back off the crossbar. Another certain point was stopped by Davey, popping up in his own back line to help out, making a courageous block.

Then there was what everybody would later simply call 'the save'.

The Newtown full-forward hit a shot on the turn. It was heading straight to the top corner of the net. Standing just metres from the kicker, Peter had already put his head in his hands preparing for the worst.

Then, out of the corner of his eye, he saw Charlie Morrissey diving. It was more than just diving. He looked like he was flying through the air with two hands outstretched in front of him.

Somehow, Charlie reached up and blocked the shot. Every player on the field was too stunned by the save to react. Except one. Peter.

'Always follow the ball in,' was another of Murph's constant reminders to his backs. Peter remembered it. This shot rebounded right into his path as he rushed towards it.

He grabbed the ball into his chest, soloed out the endline, and suddenly saw Lenny shouting for the ball.

'Peeter! Peeter!'

'Lenny, what's he doing back here?' thought Peter, looking up again just to make sure.

It was Lenny alright. Nobody else was that tall and lanky. And with Newtown forwards closing in on him from all angles, Peter was only too happy to pass.

The Lithuanian kid plucked the ball from over his head, bounced it once, and then hit a booming fist-pass down the field. It bounced right into the path of Davey who'd started sprinting forward the moment Charlie made the save. He was straight in front of the goal but surely, too far out to score.

'There's no time to pass,' thought Davey, 'I have to give it a try.'

He pulled his leg back and gave it everything

he had. It was high but not quite long enough.
The ball dropped on the edge of the square. But
before the full-back could get there, it bounced
back up again, over his head and crept over the
bar. A point. A flukey point. But the winning
point. Dromtarry were in the final.

Once the final whistle went and the celebrations started, there was more amazing stuff to
follow. As the Dromtarry players started to
walk from the field, they saw their opponents
lined up in a guard of honour at the gate. All the
Newtown players. All of their coaches. Some of
the parents too.

'What are they doing?' asked Davey.

'I think they are going to clap us off,' said
Peter.

'How do you know that?'

'I saw it once in a rugby match on television.'

'Why are they doing it?'

'I don't know. I suppose they feel sorry for
us.'

And clap is exactly what Newtown did. They

clapped loud and they clapped long. Some of the Dromtarry players smiled. Others went red with embarrassment as they walked through the corridor of applause and out the gate.

There, a load of Newtown men were standing around a large figure in a suit. They stopped the Dromtarry players and told them to wait for Murph. Once he arrived, there was another surprise.

'As chairman of Newtown,' said the large man in the suit who'd placed his hand on Murph's shoulder. 'I'd like to give you this gift to help ye in your battle. What happened to your club was an awful thing and we'd love to be able to do more. But in any case, here is a little something we raised ourselves.'

Murph took possession of the cheque and then the whispers started rushing through the squad.

'It's a thousand euros.'

'It's five thousand euros.'

'Ten thousand euros!'

It turned out to be two thousand. A gesture so kind Murph had tears in his eyes as he walked his players toward the bus. He wasn't the only one moved either.

'What did I tell you kids?' asked Shaun Reedy as he strolled along between Peter and Davey.

'Keep the faith,' said Peter in an attempted American accent.

'Exactly.'

'Still a long way from what we need,' said Davey.

'It's a start though.'

'Yeah, we just need a load of other people to be this generous now,' said Peter.

CHAPTER TWENTY-EIGHT

Peter and Davey were twenty metres from the entrance to the handball alley when they heard the noise. It sounded like glass breaking. And kids shouting and laughing.

'Who can that be?' asked Peter.

They'd been coming to the alley for a kickaround nearly every day that training wasn't scheduled. This was the first time they'd ever come across anybody else there before them.

'Do you think we should just skip this today?' asked Davey, kind of nervously.

'It's probably just some of the lads from the team,' said Peter.

'I don't know,' said Davey.

They moved forward tentatively, each carrying a football in their hands. Normally, they liked to punt the balls over the wall before they went in. Today, they thought better of doing that.

'Oh look who it is,' said a tall greasy-haired kid standing at the entrance. 'The Dromtarry All-Stars.'

The boy's name was Andy Hurley. He was two years older than Peter and Davey. They knew him from primary school before he moved up to secondary. They knew him as a kid to avoid.

'Let's just leave it,' said Peter. 'We'll come back tomorrow.'

'No!' said Davey. 'I want to see what they've done to our alley.'

Davey was the same size as Andy Hurley and he brushed past him in the doorway. Peter strolled in behind his friend, but with much less confidence.

The alley had been destroyed. There was fresh graffiti everywhere. Broken glass littered the floor. Three other boys with skateboards were sitting in a corner, smoking.

'Did ye do this?' shouted Davey. He was so

angry he couldn't even feel Peter tugging at his arm, begging him to leave it.

'We might have,' said one of the skateboarders.

'What if we did?' asked another. 'What's it to you?'

The three skateboarders were standing now. And Andy Hurley had joined them.

'Let's just get out of here, Davey,' said Peter.

'No, no, we won't,' said Davey. 'This is where we train now.'

'It is, is it?' asked the biggest of the skateboarders. 'What happened to your pitch?

The rest of the skateboarders all laughed out loud at the question.

'Oh yeah, the landslide,' said the biggest of them, now swinging his skateboard by the wheels as if it was a bat. 'That did for your little club. No more Gaelic football, wah, wah wah.'

He made the gesture of somebody wiping imaginary tears from his eyes and his friends laughed even louder.

That was enough for Davey. He bounced the ball once on the floor and then kicked it as hard as he'd ever kicked anything in his life. Straight at the tall, mocking skateboard kid.

Thwack!!

It hit him flush in the face and sent him reeling to the ground.

'What a shot!' shouted Peter, forgetting for a moment just how scared he was.

He soon regretted being so loud as the other three rushed towards Peter and Davey and jumped them. Soon, they were all in a tangle on the floor. Punches and kicks were being thrown. Hair was even being pulled.

Outnumbered four to two, Peter and Davey were coming off worst. Several digs in the ribs had left Peter winded and trapped beneath the whole scrum. Davey was better able to fight back but he was bleeding heavily from a cut lip and now had both his arms caught behind his back by Andy Hurley. The biggest skateboarder was just getting ready to punch him too.

'What the—'

Peter couldn't see who was shouting, but he knew immediately from the accent that it was Shaun Reedy. Just in the nick of time, the American was dragging the skateboard kids up and away by the scruff of the neck and pushing them back against the wall

'You are the tough guys, huh? Four against two? Is that what you call a fair fight? How about four against one? You want some of that?'

He was talking right into their faces and, suddenly, the skateboard kids had lost their appetite for fighting. They didn't look so tough anymore now that Shaun Reedy was shouting at them.

'I'm guessing you guys broke all this glass too. Am I right?'

They nodded their heads.

'I thought so. Just give me a minute then.' From somewhere inside a hole in one of the walls, he produced two sweeping brushes and a bucket.

'I want all this glass gone. Immediately!'

The skateboarders set to work, and Peter and Davey smiled from ear to ear. Not what Shaun Reedy wanted to see either.

'Outside, you two.' Peter and Davey walked outside and into a severe talking-to of their own.

'You guys should know better than to be getting involved in something like this. You're smart kids. You should have walked away and called me or Murph.'

'That's what I wanted to do,' said Peter.

'I don't care who wanted what. You don't get involved in stuff like this. You guys could have been hurt.'

'I am hurt,' said Peter, rubbing his side where his ribs already pained him.

'I mean even worse. What if one of you broke a hand or a finger? You'd have missed the final.'

'It wouldn't matter that much,' said Davey, 'because the final might be the last match we ever play as Dromtarry!'

'That's just stupid talk,' said Shaun Reedy. 'Dromtarry will be fine. You'll be fine. It's all going to work out. Now, as soon as those thugs have finished cleaning up, let's get in there and have practice.'

'We call it "training",' said Davey.

'So you do,' said the American. 'So you do.'

CHAPTER TWENTY-NINE

Peter and Davey knew something was up when their parents told them a team meeting had been called for Murph's house. They had never been to Murph's house before. Now they were walking up the street towards it wondering what was going on.

'Shouldn't we be training?' said Davey.

'Maybe this is a meeting about tactics,' said Peter

'Or the end of the club,' said Davey, still worried that the worst news was yet to come.

'Naw, I'd have heard my mum and dad talking about that,' said Peter, still trying his best to be optimistic.

When they arrived at number 52 Donovan's Road, most of the squad were already lined up along the footpath waiting for the door to open. When it did, they got a surprise. Shaun Reedy appeared in the doorway.

'Welcome, welcome, welcome,' he said. 'Please join us in the living room to the left where your coach awaits you.'

Murph was sitting in an armchair, with a smile on his face and a remote control in his hand.

'Great to see ye lads. I suppose you are wondering why we called ye here.'

A few of them nodded their heads.

'Don't worry. It's nothing to do with the club as such. It's just a story Shaun here wants to tell you.'

They sprawled all over the couches and floor as Shaun Reedy stood in front of them. For once, he wasn't smiling. He looked different, kind of nervous as he hopped from foot to foot, shuffling sheets of paper in his hand. Without even looking up, he began to read from what looked like notes.

'Okay guys, first of all I think it's important to tell you that I'm a professional football player.'

'In the Premier League?' shouted Charlie Morrissey.

'Nope. A different kind of footballer. In the

NFL back home in America.'

'You mean the one with the funny helmets where you throw the ball up in the air and try to catch it,' said Johnny Delaney, always looking for a laugh.

'That's the one Johnny,' said Shaun Reedy, always willing to play along. 'The very one.'

Peter nudged Davey. Davey nudged Peter back even harder. They knew what was coming. It had to be the story of the kick.

'Anyway, something bad happened to me once in a big game. So bad indeed that afterwards I left home and came here, because, because ... I wasn't sure if I ever wanted to kick a ball again.'

He paused as if waiting for another interruption that didn't come.

'I came here looking to hide out for a while. I wanted to get away from America and this was the only place I knew that might be safe. See, my father left this town and was gone for forty years but the town never seemed to leave him.

A while back he got sick and when he was dying, he would remember his childhood here and every memory still brought a smile to his face and a sparkle to his eyes. I don't know whether it was listening to all those stories or what, but the moment I drove through here a couple of months back I felt like I was coming home. Everybody treated me like the son of a townie.'

'Even if you do talk kind of funny,' said Johnny Delaney, just loud enough for the other kids to snigger.

'I do talk funny Johnny, but I've been trying to learn. I've learned other stuff too. Stuff that you guys have taught me. See, you reminded me of everything I used to love about sport. The way you are always smiling in the dressing-room. The way you support each other through thick and thin. The way you look out for each other on the field and off it. The way everybody in the town loves the club. The way the shopkeeper loves to talk about the games you've played and the ones you've got coming up.'

He stopped then. For a second, it almost looked like he was going to cry. But he didn't.

'Look, I just wanted to say that the way you've reacted to what happened to your field is about the bravest thing I've ever seen. The way you've kept going as a bunch of kids is unbelievable. They way you've kept training even if it was in the handball alley was inspiring. And I want to show you something now, something from my life. And I want to show you this because this was a time when people didn't react the way they should have when things went wrong.'

There was another pause but this time an interruption came.

'Are you going to show us you missing that kick now?' asked Peter. The words were out of his mouth before he could stop himself.

Shaun Reedy's face turned a brighter shade of red.

'How did you know about that?'

'We Googled you. And YouTubed you then.'

Shaun Reedy smiled and shook his head. 'So you've known all along.'

'We all know,' said Charlie Morrissey. 'We have NASN here you know and the game was live on Sky Sports too that night, but my Dad made me go to bed before it was over.'

'Your Wikipedia page is *long*,' said Davey, getting in on the act.

'You sons of guns!' said Shaun Reedy.

He began to laugh out loud and all the boys joined in.

'Well, I'm still going to make you watch this.'

CHAPTER THIRTY

Murph pressed the button on the remote and suddenly the Dromtarry Under-11s revisited the worst night of Shaun Reedy's life. This time, there was one slight difference.

As the DVD showed him warming up on the sideline, they quickly noticed something was missing.

'There's no commentary,' complained Charlie Morrissey.

'For good reason,' said Shaun Reedy. 'I don't need to relive that.'

As he began his run-up to take the kick onscreen, the entire squad began a chorus of 'Oooooohhhhhhhhing.' They were pretending to try to put him off and adding a comic air to the drama.

When the ball tailed off wide, there was the briefest moment of silence. Nobody knew what he expected them to say next. Suddenly the stillness was broken by Johnny Delaney throwing himself on to the floor with his head in his hands, perfectly imitating Shaun Reedy's position on the telly.

Within seconds, just about the whole squad had copied him and they were all writhing around the floor in mock agony.

Shaun Reedy stood by the fireplace and didn't move. He just shook his head and grinned. Of all the reactions, this was the last he expected.

'I don't believe you guys. I don't believe you,' he said.

'Put it on again! Put it on again!' said Johnny Delaney.

Shaun Reedy looked to Murph and nodded his approval. So they watched it again. And again. And again. They kept laughing at all the wrong times and they still found it hilarious every time somebody threw themselves to the carpet at the end.

Finally, Shaun Reedy took the remote and

froze the frame just at the point where he lay on the grass, alone in the middle of the packed stadium, on the biggest night of his life. His grin was gone and he had a serious face on.

'The whole point of watching this was to show you how team-mates *shouldn't* react when things go wrong for a player. Look at this picture. Look closely at it. What do you notice here?'

'Nobody comes near you,' said Davey.

'Not a single one,' said Peter.

'Exactly. None of my colleagues came to me as I lay on that field. They just walked away.'

There was silence in the room now. A bunch of ten and eleven-year-old boys as quiet as they'd been since their first days in school.

Some were nodding their heads. Others pursing their lips. All were beginning to see his point.

'Let me ask you all a question,' said Shaun Reedy. 'My kick missed by inches. What if it had went the other side of the post? How many of my team-mates would have come to me then?'

'They all would have,' said Peter.

'Wouldn't they have carried you off the field on their shoulders?' asked Davey.

'I expect they would have because that's what usually happens,' said Shaun Reedy.

He paused and hoped the lesson was sinking in.

'What can we all learn from this?' he asked.

'To try to make sure the ball goes the right side of the posts,' said Johnny Delaney, looking for and receiving yet more laughs.

'Yes, that. But what other lesson is there?'

'Support your team-mates and be there for each other no matter if you win or lose,' said Davey. He always sounded so mature when he spoke about the game.

'I think I know now what you meant by the stuff you put on the wall!' said Peter, standing up as if excited by the discovery.

'What wall?' asked Shaun Reedy.

'At training, that day just after your first joined up with us.'

'Oh, yeah,' said Shaun Reedy, suddenly remembering his attempt to inspire with slogans.

'There is no "I" in team,' said Peter. 'There is no "I" in team.'

He repeated it, because he loved the fact that he understood it now.

Shaun Reedy smiled at that. So did Murph who was now out of his chair and walking towards the double doors that led to his kitchen.

'In here lads,' said Murph. 'We've put together a little something to say thanks for all you've done getting to the final.'

When he opened the doors fully, a cheer went up.

The kitchen table was piled high with cakes and biscuits and chocolate bars. A side table was stacked with two-litre-bottles of Coke and Seven-Up.

'This ain't exactly the breakfast of champions,' said Shaun Reedy, 'but as you all like to say, dig in.'

CHAPTER THIRTY-ONE

Five minutes before the start of the last training session before the final, Davey noticed something missing from the handball alley. Not so much a thing as a person.

'Where's Shaun,' he asked Murph.

'Eh, Shaun, Shaun is gone,' said Murph. He spoke in a low voice as if he didn't want anybody else to hear.

'Gone? Gone where,' shouted Davey. He didn't mean to shout. He didn't even know he was shouting. He just couldn't help it. He was alarmed.

'Just gone,' repeated Murph.

'Will he back for Saturday? Will he back for the final?' asked Davey. His voice was still raised and it was cracking the way it always did when he was scared.

'I'm sorry to say he won't be, Davey. He won't. He's gone home.'

'He's gone home? Home to America? But why?

'Is it because we laughed at him,' asked Peter who'd walked over to the pair of them the moment he heard Davey shouting.

'We were only joking,' said Johnny Delaney as more players now gathered around Murph looking for answers.

'It's nothing to do with anything ye did or said lads,' said Murph. He was trying to sound calm and cool as the boys sounded more and more anxious. They fired off questions one and after another.

'Will he back for the final?'

'He has to come back for the final, doesn't he?'

'What about there being no "I" in team?'

'What about standing by your team-mates?'

'Through thick and thin?'

'He's gone back to his own team lads,' said Murph. 'To his job. To his life.' He was trying to sound logical, but they weren't too impressed by adult logic just then.

'I thought he lost the job when he missed the kick,' said Davey.

'I thought he hated all of them because of how they treated him,' said Peter.

'Lads, it's like this,' said Murph, his hands clasped behind his head as if searching for words. 'Tomorrow is the first day of training camp for his club, the New York Giants, in America. He has to turn up for that or he'll be sacked. So he left for Shannon early this morning.

'How could he do this to us?' asked Davey, looking around him as the rest of his pals nodded in agreement.

'It's his job, lads. It's what he trained all his life to do. He had to go back sometime.'

'Some team-mate he proved to be,' said Davey.

'Davey! Lads!,' said Murph, using an angry voice these players had never heard before. 'He owed ye nothing. He owed us nothing. He came in here and he gave me a hand for a few weeks and we were glad to have him. But he never said he was staying.'

'He never said he *wasn't* staying,' said Peter.

Murph just shook his head. He always knew it was going to be hard to break the news of Shaun Reedy's departure. He didn't think it was going to be this hard.

'I know it's upsetting. I know you were all fond of him and I know he was desperately fond of ye.'

'Not that fond of us,' said Johnny Delaney, kicking a ball off the wall to show his anger.

'Sometimes, lads, real life intrudes on us all. Shaun Reedy is a professional footballer. It's how he pays his bills and he's bloody well paid for doing it too. He couldn't be hanging around Dromtarry forever. Everybody has a job to do.'

'He might have stayed for the final,' said Davey.

'Believe me, he would have loved to have stayed for the final, but he has a contract. The club tells him when he comes to work. He doesn't tell them.'

'He could have at least told us he was going, came here to say goodbye,' said Peter.

'I don't think he could face saying goodbye to ye because a part of him wanted to stay here,' said Murph.

There was silence then for about a minute. Not even a whisper rippled through the group. Some of them were staring straight past Murph. More were looking at the ground. All seemed to be trying to take in the shock of the new information.

The trance was finally broken by Murph bouncing a ball off the ground.

'Now, lads, we have a final less than forty-eight hours away. I don't want to do too much tonight, but I want to do a bit. Are we ready to get back to work?'

Without saying anything, they began moving as if to start training. But Murph wasn't happy with that response.

'Are we ready to get back to work?'

'Yes.' This time enough of them answered for him to blow his whistle and start breaking them up into groups.

'You know what really bugs me?' said Davey to Peter as they walked over to one corner of the handball alley.

'What?' asked his friend.

'So much for Shaun Reedy telling us to keep the faith. He never cared what happened to us or this club.'

'I guess not,' said Peter, 'I guess not.'

CHAPTER THIRTY-TWO

When the bus pulled into the car park of Newtown Rangers' club, the players gasped.

'There must be five hundred people here,' said Peter as he rubbed the window to get a better look.

'Are they all here for us?' asked Davey. He sounded nervous, like he wasn't thrilled to see such a large crowd gathering for the final.

'Who else would they be here for?' asked Johnny Delaney who sounded absolutely thrilled at the prospect of playing to a large gallery.

'Look at the pitch lads, look at the pitch,' said Murph, pointing out the front window.

The final was being played at Rangers' number one pitch. With embankments running all the way around, it was usually reserved for senior teams.

For this final, smaller goalposts had been brought in to shorten the field, but with the sidelines freshly painted and properly flagged it looked perfect.

'The pitch is like something you'd see on the telly,' said Peter.

'There are our parents,' said Davey, nodding towards where the McCarthys and the O'Connors were standing together, leaning on golf umbrellas.

'I think Michael Lyster is over there,' said Johnny Delaney.

'You're only messing, he is not,' said Peter.

'I don't know about that, but I think I see our friend Megatron,' said Davey.

In the distance, they could see the largest eleven-year-old in the world was already leading his team through the gate and onto the field. The other Kilturk players looked like an army of ants walking behind him.

'He hasn't got any smaller,' said Davey.

'He looks like he's the manager of the team,

not the captain,' said Peter.

'Remember, lads, it's not the size of the dog in the fight, it's the size of the fight in the dog,' said Murph, leaning in between them.

'And we are a little bit bigger than the last time we met,' said Davey. 'Aren't we, Lenny?'

The Lithuanian strolled to the front of the bus, smiling. Murph had told him at the end of the final training session he'd be starting a Dromtarry game for the first time. And he was excited.

'My mother, she is here,' he said. 'Over there somewhere.'

'In his hands, he was carrying the number 23 jersey like it was a precious object. Murph had offered him 14 but he wanted to stay with 23.

'It is LeBron jersey you see, LeBron James is my favourite,' he'd explained. Murph didn't know who Lebron was but he played along.

And Lenny was the story of the first half of the final. The very sight of him walking onto the field seemed to unnerve the Kilturk players.

They didn't know how to cope with somebody of his size, somebody the same height as their very own 'Tank'.

The only problem was Lenny had forgotten everything he'd learned over the past few weeks. Maybe it was nerves. Perhaps it was his mother coming to see him play for the first time. But he just kept making mistakes.

Every one of his fist-passes was either too high or too long. His attempts to run with the ball were so disastrous the Kilturk goalkeeper shouted that he was like a Johnny Longlegs. Luckily, Lenny had never heard of that insect.

'*Priedurnis*!' Lenny shouted after the ref blew him up for overcarrying. Nobody knew what the word meant, but they knew it didn't mean anything good in Lithuanian.

'Mind your language,' warned the ref and Lenny nodded, but soon he was in trouble again. He tried to sneak a basketball-style pass to Johnny Delaney and gave away another free.

'Hang in there Lenny,' said Murph from the

sideline. 'Just try to relax. If you hold on to it, they'll foul you.'

He couldn't relax and pretty soon, he couldn't hold on to the ball either. His confidence was so shattered he'd even forgotten how to catch the ball properly. Passes he'd normally have plucked from the air were rebounding off his hands and into the grateful arms of Kilturk defenders.

Meanwhile, at the other end of the field, Megatron was pushing Kilturk on. He'd obviously been told not to worry about passing to the smaller players around him because as half-time approached, he'd scored all of his team's six points and Dromtarry had yet to snag even one.

'Tank, Tank, Tank,' chanted a group of Kilturk supporters from behind the goal he was attacking.

'What am I supposed to do with the kick-outs?' asked Charlie Morrissey as Peter handed him the ball behind the goalposts. 'Everywhere

I kick it Megatron catches it.'

'How about a short one?' asked Peter.

'Murph hates short ones.'

'It's either that or kick it straight to Megatron again.'

'Okay.'

Peter ran twenty metres to his left and, with no Kilturk forward near him, Charlie chipped it straight into his hands. Davey saw what was happening and made a run to help out his friend. Six passes later, Dromtarry were within scoring range.

Lenny came running out from the square with his hands in the air, calling for a pass but the ball was directed towards Johnny Delaney instead. He scooped it off the ground as it bounced and curled over a point just as the half-time whistle went.

'Six points to one,' said Davey as he trudged off the field alongside Peter. 'They're all over us.'

Peter just nodded. For once he had nothing to say.

CHAPTER THIRTY-THREE

There was no talking in the dressing-room. Nobody had anything to say. Not Davey. Not Peter. Not even Johnny. And he could never keep his mouth shut.

After what seemed like forever, Murph came in and closed the door.

'Okay, lads, has everybody had a drink of water and a piece of orange?' he asked. They barely responded. It was like they'd already lost the match.

'All right, all right. I want you to stand up off your seats and come around me in a circle.' With very little enthusiasm, they shuffled their feet and did as he asked.

'Forget the first half,' he said, punching his right fist into his left hand. 'It's over. We can't do anything about that now. But there's a second game starting shortly out there and we can win that.'

He looked around but the defeated expressions on their faces hadn't changed any.

'Kilturk won the first half by five points. We have to win the second by six. That's all we have to do and the trophy is ours.'

Again, Murph looked around. Again, there was very little response. In over 40 years managing teams, he'd never seen a squad look so down at half-time. It was like they'd given up. It was like they were drained by the events of the past few weeks. He didn't know what to say next to try to gee them up.

'Murph let me in, let me in, let me in,' said a voice shouting from outside and knocking excitedly on the door. 'It's me, Paudie, you have to let me in!'

Murph opened the door and Paudie almost fell through it. He was breathless and barely able to speak.

'Just give me a second … I've … I've … I've run all the way from the sideline.'

That broke the ice. The sight of their

favourite shopkeeper sweating and wheezing made the entire squad forget their troubles for a second. A few of them even smiled.

'Okay, I want you all to listen to this,' said Paudie. 'It's a phone message, the sound isn't great so you'll have to gather around the table.'

He placed his mobile in the centre of the table and they all stared at it like it was a bottle about to give up its genie.

'Hi guys,' went the voice on the phone. Two words that were enough to give the accent away. Shaun Reedy.

'I hope Paudie has got to you on time with this. Hopefully it's halftime now and I hope things are going well.'

The players made so much noise at that statement that Paudie gave out to them because he had to start the message again. This time they listened in almost perfect silence.

'Guys, I just wanted to say I'm sorry I didn't get a chance to say goodbye to you all and to thank you. I didn't think I was ever going to come back here to the New York Giants, but it's partly down to you guys that I did. See, you gave me the most fun couple of months I've had in a very long time. You showed me what sport should be about. You reminded me of what I loved about games all my life and made me realise how much I'd forgotten that along the way. You also taught me how it would be so wrong to quit just because I missed one kick. I can't give up on a career because of one set-back.'

In the dressing-room the only sound was breathing.

'Where would Dromtarry be if you all thought like that every time things went badly? Well you don't react like that because you are a special bunch and what you have going at that club is a very special thing. Always remember that. Whether you win or lose, remember playing for your town and for your friends and for the club your fathers and grandfathers played for is just so special. Very few people in the world get to enjoy it. Very few people get to experience it ...'

Everybody was hanging on every word. Nobody dared moved a muscle in case their boots would squeak on the floor and make it hard to hear. The voice continued.

'... I've travelled all over the planet and I've never been anywhere as unique as Dromtarry. You are kids now and you will only realise what that truly means when you get older. Anyway, I know you have the second half of a game to play and I know big Tank or Megatron or whatever we're calling him today is waiting out there, but before you go, I've something to tell you. It doesn't matter whether you win the game or lose it because the important thing is that after everything that happened you are still playing it. You still reached the final. You are still representing your club and your town.'

They were smiling now. Kind of embarrassed smiles and starting to make some noise too.

'Will you shush, he has more to say,' said Paudie.

'I know you've all been worried about the future of the club, but you can stop worrying about that now too ...'

He paused then. It was like he knew when leaving the message that a bunch of boys would make noise when they heard that.

'What does he mean?' asked Davey.

'What's happened?' asked Peter.

'Sssshhhh and you'll hear,' shouted Paudie.

'I wanted you guys to be the first to know that on Monday, work will begin on the reconstruction of the clubhouse, the dressing rooms and the field. I know this because last night I wired the money from my account here to the club account. Everything has been paid for.'

There was whooping and hollering then. Everybody was jumping around and hugging like they'd already won the final. Paudie had been smart enough to pause the message to allow for the celebrating.

'There's one more part of the message,' said Paudie, after order had finally been restored. 'Do you want to hear it?'

'Yessss!!!' They answered with what seemed like a war cry.

'Guys,' said Shaun Reedy's voice. 'I think you have to go out now and win a trophy so we can make it guest of honour at the reopening of the club.'

Murph sat back on a bench, watched his players rush through the door at top speed and then, very slowly, he wiped a tear from his eye.

CHAPTER THIRTY-FOUR

Walking back onto the pitch, every Dromtarry player suddenly felt a foot taller. They wore the big, broad grins of a team that was leading, not trailing, by five points. The Kilturk boys didn't know what was going on as their opposite numbers strolled towards them, smiling, before the ball was even thrown in.

Inspired by Shaun Reedy's phone call, Davey won the throw-in, powered forward and kicked a point. Now, only four separated the sides.

'A whole different game,' he shouted at the rest of his team as he jogged back out the field. 'Whole new game.'

They all got the message. Revved on by Davey hoovering up everything around the middle, leading by example as usual, Dromtarry tore into Kilturk for the next fifteen

218

minutes. They cut the lead to just one point. They were playing with such ferocity not even Tank was able to hold onto the ball. There were times he started to look smaller than Davey when the two of them competed for high balls.

'Keep it up, keep it up,' shouted Murph. He'd barely moved from the same spot on the side-line since the start of the second half. Until something happened that sent him rushing onto the field.

Davey had been chasing down a loose ball out near the sideline when he slipped. He still slid in to make the catch but as he did so Tank came flying in too. He knocked the ball out of his hands with one knee and followed through into Davey's ribs with the other.

'That's a foul ref, that's a foul,' shouted Murph, running towards his player.

'He meant that, every inch of it,' shouted Paudie Sweeney from behind the fence.

The ref saw no foul and ignored the shouts. Tank cruised down the field to score an easy point and Davey lay gasping for breath on the grass. By the time the ball went over the bar, Murph was kneeling by his side.

'Are you okay, Davey?' he asked.

Davey just nodded his head and wheezed

'Sit up and try to catch a breath.'

Davey obeyed the request and finally managed to speak

'My ribs are killing me,' he said.

'I've a spray here for you.' Before Davey knew it, Murph had stuck a can of something under his jersey and was squirting cold liquid onto him.

'That's freezing,' he shouted

'It'll help.'

It did help, but not enough. With his ribs throbbing, Davey got to his feet and jogged back into position. But he couldn't quite match his earlier heroics. And, even worse, Tank had come back into the game for Kilturk too.

'Tank! Tank! Tank!' The usual cheer went up.

After swapping more scores, Kilturk was still

leading by two points and the biggest eleven-year-old in the world was the reason why.

Davey had managed four of Dromtarry's points but none since the knee in the ribs.

'How much is left, ref? asked Davey as he waited for Charlie Morrissey to kick the ball out.

'Less than a minute, son,' replied the ref.

The kick-out came flying toward the spot where Davey and Tank were standing. Somehow, Davey got to it first and clutched it close to his chest. He shrugged off the huge arm reaching in to try to steal it, tried to ignore the searing pain in his ribs, and began soloing away. He could hear the heavy breathing of his huge opponent chasing him down.

'Just let it go, let it go,' shouted Murph. Amid all the noise, Davey heard the instruction and obeyed.

He put his head down and boomed the ball high and long towards the Kilturk goal.

It dropped in front of the square where six different players were waiting. After much jostling, the long arms of Lenny grabbed it. And then an amazing thing happened.

The Kilturk backs all backed off. They knew Dromtarry needed a goal to win. They knew Lenny had trouble kicking the ball so every one of them moved away to block what they assumed would have to be a pass.

'He'll have to fist it,' shouted one player.

'He can't kick the ball,' shouted another.

'Just don't give away a penno,' shouted their goalkeeper.

Lenny didn't know what to do next. All of his team-mates were covered. There was only one option left. To everybody's surprise, he turned towards goal and with nobody near enough to try to stop him, he pulled back his right leg and attempted a shot.

Miraculously, he managed to connect with his right boot. It wasn't a perfect strike. It wasn't even a very good strike. But, somehow, it was enough. The ball hit the ground in front of the Kilturk keeper. A bounce. One very, very lucky bounce that took the ball a metre to the right and just out of the goalie's reach.

'*Phreeeep!*'

The final whistle went as the ball trickled into the back of the net. Dromtarry had won it right at the death.

Lenny fell to his knees with his arms in the air as if too shocked to move. Within seconds, he disappeared beneath a scrum of team-mates.

'Make room for one more,' shouted Peter. He'd run the length of the field to join in the celebrations. He landed on top of the pile, just beside his best friend in the world.

'Keep the faith,' shouted Davey as they hugged.

'Keep the faith,' shouted Peter right back at him.

Then they both started laughing uncontrollably.

CHAPTER THIRTY-FIVE

'It looks good, doesn't it?' said Davey.

'It's so shiny,' said Peter.

'I know, my mum polished it this morning.'

'We can see ourselves in it from here.'

'It's bigger than I thought it would be too.'

'Much, much bigger.'

Peter and Davey were sitting on the front room floor in the McCarthy's house. They were staring up at the mantelpiece over the fire. A mantelpiece that was now decorated by the large silver cup Dromtarry had won the day before.

'Is everything ready for what we planned?' asked Peter.

'I think so, I've been at this game all morning,' replied Davey.

'Really?'

'Yeah, I even had to ask my dad to help.'

They were talking about Madden '09, the

Wii game on the television screen in front of them. Just half an hour before his friend arrived, Davey had frozen the action in the match. A match he'd started the moment he got up that morning. Even before he ate breakfast.

'It's taken you that long?' asked Peter.

'Yeah, it was harder than I thought.'

'And the score is right?

'Yeah, I even double-checked all the details on Wikipedia.'

Davey had frozen the game with just three seconds left on the clock in the fourth quarter. He'd frozen it with the New York Giants trailing 21-20 to the Buffalo Bills. He'd frozen it at the exact spot where the Giants' kicker Shaun Reedy is called in to take a field goal to win the game. Not just any game, of course. To win the Super Bowl.

'What happens if he misses again?' asked Peter.

'He won't. I've been using the mini-games to practise my kicking motion.'

'Are you sure?'

'I'm sure. Besides, this is slightly nearer than the kick he missed that night. I couldn't quite fix the yardage.'

Davey looked as serious as he did when taking frees from Dromtarry. His brow was wrinkled and his eyes narrowed. Only one difference. He was now holding the Wii remote in his hand rather than getting ready to kick an O'Neill's football. He had the A button pressed down and the remote pulled back and poised to strike.

'Will I restart then? Are you ready?' asked Peter.

'Yeah … no, no … hang on.'

'What is it?'

'You better just make sure I'm recording it as a highlight.'

'Oh yeah, good thinking.' Peter did the necessary. It was all systems go.

'You know it's the same commentary team on this that we heard doing the real game on

YouTube,' said Davey.

'Really?'

'Yeah, the same fellas.'

'Let's hope they don't jinx him.'

They were both standing up now. They were both ready to give Shaun Reedy another chance with the kick that changed his life. The commentary began.

'*...with three seconds remaining, it falls to New York Giants' place-kicker Shaun Reedy. If he can convert this field goal, he will win his team the world championship ... The ball is snapped ...*'

At that point, Davey swung the remote forward in the same kicking motion he'd been practicing on and off for hours.

'*He's kicked it ... It has the height ... It looks good ... It is good, good, good ... It's great ...The Giants win the Super Bowl. The Giants win the Super Bowl ... And Shaun Reedy has disappeared beneath a pile of his team-mates ...*'

By that point in the commentary, Peter and Davey were jumping around the living room with their hands in the air. They were making so much noise celebrating that Mrs McCarthy popped her head in to check on them.

'What are you two up to now?' she asked. They didn't need to answer. She looked at the screen and laughed. 'I take it your friend scored this time then?'

'Yes, he did!' shouted Davey.

'Right between the posts,' said Peter not quite as loudly.

'Well I'm happy for him and for ye,' said Mrs McCarthy.

'Wait 'til you see what we are going to do next,' said her son.

'And what's that?' asked Mrs McCarthy

'We're uploading this highlight onto You-Tube,' said Peter

'Why?' she asked.

Mrs McCarthy didn't understand that part of the plan. She figured the Wii experiment was just their bizarre way of paying tribute to their American friend.

'So everyone can see him making the kick this time,' said her son.

'And maybe even Shaun Reedy himself will see it,' said Peter.

'And?' asked Mrs McCarthy, still bemused by the whole game.

'He'll see that it was uploaded by us,' said Peter.

'And?' She still wasn't quite getting the point.

'And this is our way of saying thanks to him for everything he did for us,' said Davey.

His mother nodded and smiled. Now, at last, she understood.

**Have you read the books about GAA player
Danny Wilde?**

**Turn the page to read an extract from *Little Croker*,
the first book about Danny Wilde and his team, the
Littlestown Crokes ...**

The Match Against
St Agnes' Boys

Mick Wilde's boys, in all-blue, lined up against the boys in red and green from St Agnes' Boys. Each player, from Paddy Timmons at right corner full back to Danny in midfield, right up to Doyler in full forward, anxiously awaited the throw-in.

Mick tied Heffo's lead to his bag and began his routine pacing up and down the line, while Jimmy just stood with his arms folded looking relaxed.

'Here we go,' announced Jimmy.

'Come on the Crokes!' shouted Mick.

'Ready, lads?' asked the ref.

Then he gave Danny and the St Agnes'

midfielder a nod. Danny and his opposite number raised their heads as the referee blew on his whistle and threw the ball high above them.

Danny was first in the air stretching his left hand above his opponent's. He passed the ball down to Sean Dempsey, then turned his man and headed for goal, leaving the St Agnes' number nine dazed with Danny's pace. The battle had commenced!

Dempsey kicked straight up to Barry Sweeney in centre half forward, who knocked a perfect pass out to Splinter Murphy.

Splinter threw a shimmy around his man and spotted Danny running in behind the full forward line.

Danny raised his hand.

Doyler made a run wide and opened up a gap for Danny.

Splinter knocked a sweet pass in towards Danny, who caught it beautifully on the run.

Danny took a quick glance at goal and

dropped the ball onto the side of his right boot.

The ball swerved past their keeper and into the top right corner.

GOAL!

'Come on, lads!' shouted Danny as he fisted the air in glorious celebration.

Mick and Jimmy were hopping around on the side line.

'What a dream start!' cheered Jimmy.

'Come on lads, settle down and back into it!' warned Mick.

Jimmy was right – Danny had given the Crokes the perfect dream start and it totally rattled the St Agnes' boys.

Barry Sweeney caught the kick out and knocked a long, high ball over for a point.

Crokes kept the ball in St Agnes' end of the field for the next twenty minutes, scoring four more points. Danny was playing a stormer in midfield, winning everything in the air and when they tried to break through, Danny relentlessly pulled off tackle after tackle.

When the ref blew for half time the Crokes
were winning 1-5 to nil.

Little Croker by Joe O'Brien ISBN: 978-1-84717-0460